"NEVER PLAY LEAPFROG WITH A UNICORN"

..a coming of age slice
of a farcical life..

Note for Librarians: A cataloguing record for this book is available from Library
and Archives Canada at www.collectionscanada.ca/amicus/index-e.html

Printed in Victoria, BC, Canada.

ISBN: 978-1-4120-1305-5 (Soft)
ISBN: 978-1-4122-1742-2 (e-book)

*We at Trafford believe that it is the responsibility of us all, as both individuals
and corporations, to make choices that are environmentally and socially sound.
You, in turn, are supporting this responsible conduct each time you purchase a
Trafford book, or make use of our publishing services. To find out how you are
helping, please visit www.trafford.com/responsiblepublishing.html*

*Our mission is to efficiently provide the world's finest, most comprehensive
book publishing service, enabling every author to experience success.
To find out how to publish your book, your way, and have it available
worldwide, visit us online at www.trafford.com*

Trafford rev. 10/16/2009

 www.trafford.com

North America & international
toll-free: 1 888 232 4444 (USA & Canada)
phone: 250 383 6864 ♦ fax: 812 355 4082 ♦ email: info@trafford.com

Acknowledgements

To the writers, the poets, the readers, the membership at **fanStory.com**. I came to this writers den, this vast readers haven, in search of writing knowledge, of approval & encouragement. I found an audience.

To my lifeline: Christine, Monika, Lindsey, Rachel, Max & Chris.

To Terry Burke & her immediate family: Lily, Mickey, Henry & Pooh Bear, for lending an ear, computer, printer, ink & mouse, the plastic one.

To Roy Baltozer: for listening, laughing, for your encouragement over these many years.

To Jo-An Thomas: for your wisdom, for your truth, for believing in my story.

To Harry Harris: for your humor, frustration, friendship, & fielding my many questions.

To my readers, my friends, my many thanks: Lisa Cook, Ron Gordon, Jen Kiernan, Sean Casey, Harriet Thorpe, Joe Orlando, Tami Lynch, John Parsons, Lisa Reynolds, Joe "Chuck" McGuire, Love Moran, Mike Sanchez, Dan & Melissa Williams.

Contents

My Li'l Black Dad - 11

The Family Bush - 29

A Dog By Any Other Name - 39

The Ballad of J. Dean Presley - 47

Geraldine & Erwin - 57

The Goodies Incident - 65

Home Sweat Home - 71

Me Tarzan-You Vain - 81

The Fabulous Beulah - 89

Miss Colmes Studio of Tap & Modern Jazz - 125

The Recital - 143

Miracle Patches - 155

The Blessing of the Rooms - 169

The Legal Arson - 177

The Blessing of the House - 191

Between the comedy
and the drama
dwells the dramedy.

Chapter 1

My Li'l Black Dad

When I was born, my dad was short and black.

Well, no, not quite. Let's say not "short" short, but, vertically challenged. And not "black" black, but, how about he was, uh, colored? Yes. Better. He was colored. Yes. Vertically challenged and colored. Better. Much better. He was four colors, actually.

Being I was, and still am at this writing, a certifiable Caucasian, an explanation would be in order.

You see, for many years, long before I was born and long after, my dad worked in a foundry. An iron foundry. Know what they make in iron foundries? They make, along with many other iron works, reindeer. Those cast iron "Rudolph" reindeer which set posed on rich people's front lawns.

Over time, dust, minute particles of dark, rust-orange airborne iron dust, collects in fine layers on the skin and well into the skin's pores, causing deep, dark discoloration. A change in pigmentation. All exposed skin, if not vigorously scoured and showered clean daily, will begin discoloring in a short period of time. If foundry work is what one chooses to do for an extended period, the change in skin color will be deep, dark, and long lasting.

Even though a communal shower area was available at the foundry, my dad depended on the goodwill of his fellow workers

for rides to and from work and abided by their schedule. He never had a license to drive. I never knew why.

This is not to say he never took advantage of the foundry's shower area, on occasion he did. But, being a grateful, considerate hitcher, this everyday mode of transportation more often than not meant, 5 p.m. whistle, 5 p.m. shuffle home.

On the surface, what seemed the typical end to a typical workday: get home, take a shower, eat dinner, etc., was, unfortunately, wishful thinking, as our "year-round" summer house did not come with a shower. Using the foundry's shower facilities a handful of times a month over a twenty-five, thirty year work span, was just not enough.

So, from the day I was born to the age of nine, I assumed, accepted as given fact, without question, with wide-eyed youthful innocence, I was the God-given son to a short black man.

Hey, I was nine and a half. If you're never told, whattya know?

No one, not a soul, said a word about adoption. The thought never even occurred to me. Why should it? I wasn't. Even if I were, I suspect the idea would've passed quickly, for I had more important things on my mind: Howdy Doody, The Lone Ranger, Hop-A-Long-Cassidy, The Cisco Kid, Abbott and Costello, and The Three Stooges. I could only watch the Stooges when he and I were home alone. We thought they were funny. My mother thought they were a bad influence.

Oh, all right, I watched Big Brother Bob Emery, too. But, only because my sisters liked to drink their milk and salute the flag, with kind, white-haired, Big Brother Bob, once a day, everyday. Until the day he thought his microphone was off and Big Brother Bob announced to all the little tykes in TV land: "That ought to hold the little bastards!" Shocked, my sisters choked on their milk and my mother dropped her cookies.

Where was I?

Oh, so, no one ever mentioned, made an issue of, or questioned his color. Nobody, not a soul, ever pointed out any glaring errors in my family tree. Or, "the family bush" as my li'l black dad so often referred to it.

Nobody ever said a thing to me! I repeat, if you're never told, whattya know?

Forty-seven dwellings dotted the right and left of my dead-end street. The East Lake, with its surplus of sunfish, snapping turtles, and an occasional water snake, ran along the edge of nineteen properties on the right, the rest in a haphazard, helter-skelter manner on the left, in and along the wood-line.

Of the forty-seven sites, thirty-three were definitive summer cottages. All of them no better or worse than can be found in any low-to-mid-cost cabin campground. Thirty-three drab, lifeless, forgotten shells sprang to life three months a year, when their owners fled the sizzling city heat for the cool, sultry breezes of lakeside Shangri-Las. A veritable utopia in suburbia.

Over the years, of the fourteen other dwellings, twelve were converted to realistically proportioned, storm windowed, Owens-Corning wrapped, furnace fired, foundationed, four season, year-round homes. The last two stayed exactly the same as if frozen in time. Over-sized, wind-driven, un-insulated, no heating system, cellar less, shower less, aged dinosaurs.

Though weather-beaten and battered, both year-round summer houses still stood, deformed yet defiant, after umpteen harsh, lonely New England winters, and as many raucous lakeside summers.

They stood testament to the cosmetic cover-up capabilities of gallons upon gallons of interior and exterior paint and the holding power of Spackle, troweled on layer upon layer by decades of many past owners.

Summer-loving do-it-yourselfers, home handy-men all, and just what could be done if the spirit was willing, even though the wallet was weak, on a few off-season week-ends, and three months in the summer, with a collection of sorted nails, a couple of two-by-fours, a handful of shingles, half a roll of tar-paper, a bucket of black tar, and a roll of duct tape.

Unfortunately, over the many years, and the many do-it-yourselfers' trial and errors, no two handymen shared the same idea as to what either house should end up looking like.

The "Great Gray Monster" had stood empty and spooky-looking for a very long time, sitting three house lots behind us. We lived in the other pauper's palace. The "Great White Elephant" towered in monumental tribute to the vast legion of do-it-yourselfers over many decades past.

Whenever either house was sold it went for pennies on the dollar. Both needed major work. Major extensive structural work. Major expensive structural work. This, along with repairing, replacing, gutting, and finishing years of half-baked projects and half-assed outcomes by many past well-intentioned summer owners, would have cost a pretty penny to correct.

"Makes no sense throwing good money after bad. Don't much matter, we don't have either one," my dad would say. Then he'd grin, chuckle, cough, huck a louie, fart, and walk away. All at the same time.

I tried it once when I was seven and sprained my ankle.

So, we owned the Great White Elephant but lived like renters. We did nothing to it but live in it and keep a nice lawn. This was my job. Mow the large lawn, rake the large lawn, water the large lawn, keep off the large lawn, worship the large lawn, things like that.

To make structural oddities just a bit stranger, Roger, a rugged, good-looking, red-headed Irishman, a former neighbor, occasional painting contractor and seemingly capable jack-of-all-trades, stopped by one day, while my sisters and I were in school and my

dad was at work, to visit with my mother, who did neither. You could have knocked my li'l black dad over with a feather when one Saturday, while taking the rubbish out, he discovered a good size hole dug out, along, and under the side of the house.

For two weeks, during daylight hours, Roger had been coming around and had begun digging a cellar.

Nobody could quite understand why but, suddenly, out of the blue, my mother just had to have a cellar.

My dad left for work in the morning darkness, returning in the evening darkness. He saw nothing. Heard less. He never had a chance. He was ambushed. Sideswiped. Hoodwinked. Bamboozled. Everybody knew. Even I knew!

"Surprise!" said my mother to my slack-jawed dad, as we stood looking down into the pit.

"Nobody ever said anything to me," he hollered.

'Like father, like son,' I thought. "If you're never told, whattya know?" I offered.

"If I want any shit outta you, boy, I'll squeeze your head."

He had such a way with words.

I rarely saw Roger. When he came around to dig I was in school, so I really didn't know much about him. Then again he was my mother's friend, my dad's curiosity, not mine.

One thing I did know, Roger must've loved working with dirt because he certainly wasn't being paid to do it. Unfortunately, his customers requested most painting jobs be done on the weekends. This meant Roger wasn't around when my li'l black dad was. So, on weekdays, Roger tended the hole all by himself. On the weekends, my dad would crawl in the hole alone. Not exactly sure why, or even how, he got involved in the first place.

They had to crawl under the house on their bellies and work in that position until they had dug out, and lugged out, enough dirt to

15

work on their knees, bent over. And then until they had dug a deep enough hole to squat, bent over. Then until they had dug out a pit deep enough to semi-stand, bent over. And then a crater dug deep enough to stand, bent over. All the while dragging back in logs, rocks, bricks and blocks, to shore up the aged, rotting house beams.

This went on and off, off and on, for the better part of a year. Finally, came the day when Roger had dug down deep enough to stand upright, I'll be damned if the hole didn't begin filling with water!

This was the first time I heard the term "water table" used.

I couldn't tell whether my mother didn't want to tell or didn't know how to tell my dad the "Surprise!" had sunk, because Roger kept coming around anyway. He'd clear away the leaves and re-arrange the plywood covering the entrance to the pit, along with moving around the blocks and rocks holding the plywood in place.

It appeared all was normal and Roger was taking care of business in the hole just fine.

My l'il black dad, after putting in forty to fifty hours a week at the foundry, had tired months before of digging alone, of working at all, on his week-ends off. So, as all talk of the cellar pretty much stopped, he figured he was off the hook and Roger would rather be in the hole alone anyway. He also figured Roger must like what he's doing: he's coming around three, four, sometimes five days a week, and my mother's not complaining. So, everybody was happy.

They kept their little secret to themselves for some time.

Then late one afternoon, while in my room doing my homework, I overheard my mother talking on the phone to Roger. She was laying the law down. "I can't do this anymore. He's acting funny. I know he suspects. He's not stupid. Well, goddamn it, if you don't tell him I will! What's-a-matter, lose your fucking nerve? I'm

sorry, sorry, sorry! I am. I know. I do too. I will. Soon? Promise? If you do, I'll love you forever."

She never used language like, "love you forever". This is how I knew she was afraid to break the news of the flood, alone, to my l'il black dad.

Well, wouldn't you know, out of the blue, within days of that phone call, they opened Roger up, looked in, shook their heads, closed him up, and weeks later, Roger drops dead of cancer of the whatever.

My mother cried when she told my dad. I wouldn't think a high water table and not having a cellar would make anybody cry so much. It was clear to me she was upset because she had been so close to having what she wanted, then it was snatched away. She wanted it so bad.

Damn water table!

Oddly enough, my li'l black dad seemed to walk with a spring in his step. He even seemed chipper when he heard the news. And I know why. Obviously, he wouldn't be digging a cellar, so he wouldn't be missing any of his Sox games.

This was the good news.

The bad news? The water filled the hole and kept rising, spilling over the rim of the crater, not stopping until the crawl space was full. Come winter, the muddy ice rink froze, the rag-wrapped water pipes burst, and the rotted center carry beam, weakened by all the moisture, cracked.

His step was less springy, more squishy. His once chipper mood replaced by the chip on his shoulder.

"He did it, the phuck! Go 'n wreck my house. Phucker crawl up your arse, phucker want something. Shoes on the other foot, where's the phucker now?"

"Um, he's dead, dad."

"Funny, boy. Real funny."

And, the Great White Elephant now sagged in the middle.

Downstairs was the kitchen sink, and upstairs a bathroom hand sink and an old "iron-claw" tub. Sunday night was bath night. This was the only night the tub was used, and even then never ever filled, because when filled to normal the water's weight made the old warped floorboards "pop" and "tic." My mother was convinced one day the tub would come crashing down into the living room and we would all drown. Not to mention the luckless soul sitting on the sofa, located directly beneath the tub, would be crushed.

Getting ready for school on cool New England spring mornings, chilly falls, and bitterly cold winters, I would fill up the hand sink with hot water, fold my arms, immerse them, then plunge my face in. Not having a proper heating system in my year-round summer house, this was not so much to wash-up as it was to get warm.

"Freeze the brass off a bald monkey!" my dad would say on chilly mornings.

"Freeze the balls off a brass monkey!" he'd say in the winters deep-freeze.

I thought of this as blue-collar meteorology.

I did not have any feelings one way or another, good or bad, right or wrong, towards my friends and their Caucasian Dads. I did harbor just a little resentment though when I realized not only did all of my friends have everyday usable tubs, but their houses all came with showers.

"Dad, are we too poor to have a shower?"

"You can never be too poor, boy."

"Then, are we broke?"

"Broke? I wouldn't say broke, boy. Badly bent, but not broke."

"Oh."

I was now positively convinced I am the son of a hard working, well intentioned, but poor black man, because we, because my house, not only did not have a shower, we didn't even have an everyday usable bathtub.

Everything he wore, touched, owned, reeked of iron. Years back, iron residue from his hair and skin turned my mother's bedding a deep, rusty-orange color. This just would not do. So she decided the "boys," my li'l black dad and I, would share the small bunk-bed room, and the "girls," my mother and two sisters, would share the big bedroom located across the wide-open hallway. He didn't seem to mind.

His bedding never changed. A limp, lifeless, thin pillow. An old, scratchy Army blanket. A sad, saggy, single mattress. That was it. No pillowcase, no sheets. The deep, dark, rusty discoloration of his bedding was caused by his job. However, at no time did it dawn on me, ever, at all, the color of his skin was anything but the color of his skin.

Intimacy between them never occurred to me. Whether she wouldn't or he couldn't, or vice versa, didn't seem to matter. They just didn't. Not anymore, anyway. How could they? I would've known. He slept on the bottom bunk, I was on top. This was okay with him. He couldn't share her bed. She wouldn't share his. So any show of passion between the two consisted of a cheeky peck when he left for work in the morning and once again at bedtime. That was it. That was just the way it was.

This arrangement didn't seem to bother him. Nothing seemed to bother him. Even if something did, you wouldn't know. Because all you would see was his wicked grin. And all you would hear was his fractured logic.

"I can't tell whether I'm going bald or if my arse is getting bigger pulling my forehead back!" Or, "I wouldn't know I had a hair across my arse even if I had a hair across my arse!"

Given what was to soon happen, his words now seemed quite prophetic.

My dad worked, drank, followed the Red Sox, slept, and called upon a rather crude sort of child rearing. The only conversation anyone was able to get out of him was: "Shut-up, the game's on." "Get me another beer." "Wake me so I can go to work." Or, his all time signature favorite: "Pull my finger!" But somehow, thanks to baseball, thanks to the Red Sox, we bonded.

When the need arose he was able, and did not hesitate to call on, a rather unique form of dual discipline and parental affection. This ability consisted of melding the five fingers of his right hand together to create a firm flab of functional flesh. Holding the fleshy slab at an angle favoring the point of impact, he would thrust and flick. This two-part motion had a far better end all when delivered in one, smooth, fluid stroke, taking full advantage of the strikers 3-R factor: rage, reach, and random reason.

The third "R" was also known as the surprise "R" because the reason for said blow could well be a passing moment of forgotten discipline. Surprise! Or a disguised attempt at fatherly affection. Surprise! Then again it might not have anything to do with either discipline or affection but immediate availability and convenience for release of passing momentary frustration. Surprise! Such as a Red Sox loss. Surprise! Waking him two minutes too soon. Surprise! Two minutes too late. Surprise! Or a sudden "0" level beer inventory and no one of legal age available in the home at the time to accommodate the purchasing, the replenishing, of aforementioned potable spirits. Surprise!

Although she made numerous attempts, my mother was never capable of mastering this unique form of discipline. So she would call on her old stand-by of forming a pair of fleshy fist balls and charge full tilt, fist balls flailing. Surprise factor - zero.

When the Sox were on, providing no one was in the tub, I would take my older sister's "spot" on the sofa. Come game time, this was "my" spot. My dad decreed it. My older sister hated us. My

younger sister just fell in line and went along with whatever rules my mother and older sister made up in getting through another day with him and me. It seemed like it was them against us. This was just the way it was.

His weekends never varied. Watch Sox, drink beer, scratch privates, doze off.

He would sit in "his" chair. An old, worn, black, brown, red, rust orange, blue upholstered easy chair. At the ready to his right, a metal folding tray table, holding all his worldly weekend needs. A very large soon to be overflowing, clear, glass ashtray. Three beer bottles. One empty, one full and uncapped, one half-full and in use. A metal bottle opener. Two books of matches, one unused, the other half lit. Two packs of Pall Malls®. One unopened, the other in use. Two sharpened No. 2 pencils. And a blank score sheet the old Boston Herald-Record American printed for hardcore Red Sox fans to pencil in complete games. He would score every televised game, including both games of a double-header, recording all stats, RBI's, ERA's, etc., with the acute proficiency of a sports analyst.

When the Red Sox got a hit, we'd grin. When they made an out, we'd nod and grunt. When they scored, we'd hoot. And when they hit a homer, I'd get him another beer. When the game ended, the last pitch thrown, the last out made, he'd wad the scorecard into a ball and attempt a strike at my head. If he missed, he'd grin. If I caught it, he'd nod and grunt. If he hit my head he'd hoot, and I'd get him more beer. Thinking back, whether he hit me, missed me, or I caught it, he still got beer. Surprise factor - zero.

We were bonding. Male bonding. The early years.

All his needs, all his wants, were really quite simple. A pack of Pall Malls in his pocket, a few beers with the guys at the Blue Moon on Friday, a six pack in the fridge, and three squares a day.

The rest of his paycheck my mother gingerly divvied out to umpteen creditors, neighbor markets, banks, utilities, paperboys, and the Avon lady, Mrs. Sinnott. Or, Mrs. Snot, as my mother

21

called her, 'cause of the way her nose pitched up, taking her upper lip with it.

My mother ordered cosmetic cover-ups from her, so Mrs. Snot's hand was always out. I often thought, because of my mother's large, imposing build, and Mrs. Snot, a small, frail woman, she didn't so much extend credit to my mother as a good customer, but more she was scared to death to say no. I suspected my mother was well aware of the intimidation Mrs. Snot felt because every month, my mother's request for free samples, brought a small mountain of Avon products, courtesy of Mrs. Snot.

There were too many mouths open and way too many hands out for one little paycheck. My li'l black dad was doing the best he knew how. My mother was doing her best also. Borrow, borrow, borrow, spend, spend, spend.

All kitchen chatter drifted up through the vent the kitchen ceiling shared with my bedroom floor. Tonight's topic: Money. The crux of my dad's concern: "Where the hell's it all going?"

"I'm doing the best I can," she said.

"Oh, you working?" he asked.

"Tell me, what can I do? You tell me?"

"Blue Moon always needs waitresses."

"I don't know how to waitress."

"Get me a beer."

"I have never waitressed and you know it. Here's your beer."

His point was obvious. "Anyone can serve beer!"

Whether she got it or not, didn't much matter. He made his point. I couldn't see but I know he was grinning. Like a Cheshire cat, he was grinning.

A season came. A season went. Then, on one bitterly cold winter's day, the overhead pulley system the foundry used to relay the cast iron Rudolph works in progress from one reindeer work area to the next, slipped, and just like bad magic—abracadabra—my Red Sox worshipping, blue collar, Black Horse®, Blue Ribbon®, Black Label®, li'l black dad was paralyzed, waist down.

Later, when asked what caused his life-altering disability, he would often reply, "I was taken out by Rudolph the friggen red-nosed reindeer. Ho-de-ho-de-phucken-ho-ho!"

The ambulance sped to the hospital. Emergency surgery was done, more to stabilize the obvious than cure the incurable. His left leg crushed and badly mangled, amputated. He'd become a paraplegic.

It was thought best us kids not visit him for awhile, a couple of weeks anyway. My mother went everyday, and when she got home, between the neighbors calling her and her calling the neighbors, she gave the daily updates in detail. This is how I was able to get, not understand fully, but able to get a good idea how my dad was really doing. Because when I asked how he was, she'd say, "Fine. Good." Or, "How the hell do you think he's doing?"

When my first visit was finally allowed to happen, on a cold, snow swept winters night, my mother and I went alone. On the ride to the hospital, because she, understandably, did not want him getting upset, she spoke at length, darn near lectured me, about being careful what I say. "I promise." With so much instruction and warning about what I couldn't talk about, there wasn't much left.

"How about Little League?" she asked.

"Huh?"

"Talk about Little League."

"But, it's December."

"So? You can't talk about Little League in December?"

23

"Yeah, but, I don't have, what can I--?"

"If you say one thing, one goddamn thing out of line, if you upset him, I'm telling you, you'll never talk about Little League again because there won't be any Little League to talk about. Understand? Do you understand?"

It was a cold, raw, miserable night. "The kind of night that turns virgins into whores," my dad would say. At that age, I didn't know what either was. All I know is when he said it he'd laugh, so I did too.

The weather had turned to driving rain and sleet. A freezing, pelting, winter sleet, that cut right through your clothes and nipped at your skin. The heater wire in the car was broken. It was cold outside and inside. I was an icicle.

I followed as she led me down a very long, gloomy, green corridor. As we pushed through the large ward doors, everything got much brighter and much, much warmer.

We walked down the middle of the aisle, a row of occupied beds on either side. I didn't know there would be others. I never gave a thought there would be others. Just my li'l black dad. I didn't look left or right, but, ahead. Straight ahead. I didn't look at anybody. I didn't see anybody. I didn't want to.

She stopped at the sixth bed on the right. He was asleep, face down in the pillow. She set down the carton of smokes, removed her coat, and sat in the large leather chair. I stood on the other side of the bed trying not to stare at the sheet covering his stump. She caught me trying to follow the outline of the shape of the leg which wasn't there. She shot me a look and hissed, "sssit!" The nearest chair was across the wide aisle between two beds of "others."

"I'm okay," I muttered.

She leaned over and whispered his name in his ear a few times. He turned his head to face her. Now face-to-face, she looked at him in

24

a most endearing way. I'd never seen this look. She stroked his li'l black head. Water puddles filled her eyes.

"Look who I brought to see you," she said as I sniffled.

I stepped around the foot of the bed and up the other side. He tucked his chin down and looked at me with a hazy, medicated look, and smiled.

"How you doin', boy?"

"Merry Christmas, Dad. Do you need, want anything special?" I choked.

"A sock."

And, as he lay there on that hospital bed, flat on his stomach, he shot me his best wicked grin and gurgled a belly laugh, choking on the smoke from the sideways drag he took off the Pall Mall my mother had lit and held to his mouth.

"That wasn't funny," she said.

No, it really wasn't, but try convincing my funny bone. The swallow of generic hospital ginger ale I had just taken to calm me, came back up the same route it took going down, only faster, and burst from my mouth. And, as an extra added bonus, a good amount gushed out of my nose.

"I said that wasn't funny!"

"I know, I—"

"What in hell is wrong with you? Go wait in the car!"

"But—"

"What did I just say?"

Walking to the ward doors, I glanced back just as his eyes closed, his head turned, and he drifted off, humming his favorite Christmas carol. Well, maybe not his favorite, but it was his funniest: "Chet's nuts roasting by an open fire..."

"That's not funny!"

Even if he wasn't all drugged and medicated, I know he still would not have said a word in my defense. He had all he could do standing up to her when he was whole. We had all we could do standing up to them when we were whole.

Now the playing field had narrowed considerably.

People called offering sad regrets. "God has his reasons." "Keep your chin up." "You're the man of the house now." I smiled, nodded, I know they meant well.

But what really burnt me was when my mother chimed in with her, "Well, it certainly does look like you really are the big man of the house now."

'Will you please! I just masturbated for the first time last week and I darn near bled to death from not being circumcised and pulling back too far! I've been walking around with a Band-Aid on it for days, afraid to look! I told my friends, when you're a kid you can do things like that, and they said I shouldn't be doing "that" for three or four more years! There is a very good chance I may have ruined it completely! Will you hear? I am not the big man of the house! Do you hear me?'

No, she didn't hear a word, because I couldn't say a word. Thanks to Rudolph, my world, my home, my life, is now "female censored." We never talked guy stuff, certainly never "those" things.

Conversation was nil. Censorship thrived.

"You gotta learn to grin, boy. Grin and bear it. I'm never going home again. You're the man of the house now, boy," my father said.

There were no choices offered to me and even fewer questions asked, as far as how different my life, and life in general would be now that he was gone. Well, not "gone" gone, just not here, but there.

My mother dealt with the stress and pressure of the known present, and the unknown tomorrows, about as good as she dealt with all stress-filled situations. She wanted one of us near one minute, the next minute she was flipping off the walls, ranting and raving. If we could have ranted and raved back a little, allowed to express our frustrations in some manner, it might've done us some good, it might've helped all of us. But her episodes were the only ones allowed.

As the weeks, months, and years crept by, her stress-filled rants and raves grew angrier and uglier.

It took some time for my dad to accept his new lot in life. No more a part of the rat race. No longer just another fifth grade educated laborer. Time clock puncher. Another li'l black face in the crowd. At the end of the bar. Sleeping it off on the side of the road. Or the woods. In a leaf pile. On a snow bank.

Doctors, doctors, doctors. Nurses, nurses, nurses. Orderlies, candy stripers. Needles, needles, needles. Tubing. Drugs, drugs, drugs. Meds, meds, meds. Urine bags dangling offensively. The smells of ointments, crèmes, liniments, Lysol®.

Rows of beds. Of bedridden men in sorted states of disrepair. A wheelchair bound life.

Miles and miles of freshly laundered white sheets, wrapping, covering, hiding, limbs, stumps, nubs, halves of the whole.

For the first few months I would visit daily and find those sheets, those wonderful, sparkling white sheets, pulled up to his neck,

tucked under his chin. His little black head, his little wrinkled face, center of the pillowcase. I stood staring, forbidden to wake him, per my mother's instructions.

"He needs his rest," she would say.

"I just want to talk to him."

"Well, he's resting. Go wait in the car."

How much rest does a man need? Rest was all he did. Rest was the only thing he did. How many more months of nightly visits watching him rest? Give a kid a break. Will somebody talk to me?

So, I would stand, sit, wait, stare, and compare the uncanny resemblance between my li'l black dad and a photo in an old National Enquirer newspaper of a shrunken head on a stick.

Chapter 2

The Family Bush

For the first couple of weeks many visitors came. Some I knew,
many I did not know, and a few I should've known.

My dad's drinking buddies from the Blue Moon took up a
collection and a few of them brought it over to the house. Some of
his whiter, well-showered co-workers stopped by and spoke
warmly of missing him. The canteen driver even put a spare
change can out on the shelf of his "roach-coach" for a few days
and brought it by.

The foundry owners came by with a turkey, all the fixings, and a
Christmas bonus check. They assured my mother the health
insurance would take care of everything and if there was anything,
anything at all she needed, do not hesitate to call.

Someone told her she should sue the foundry, but she said, "Those
guys are his friends and the foundry has been very good to us over
the years. Look at this. They didn't have to give us such a big
turkey."

Assorted other folks stopped by. Among them, much to my shock
and occasional curiosity over the years, my li'l black dad's older
brothers. Three well heeled, sparkling white Uncles I should have
known, but never did. I did know they were all married but I had

never met the wives, or the cousins for that matter, if I even had any.

Why? I don't know.

I did know they were well aware of their younger brother's life-long, modest existence.

My l'il black dad had been pruned from the family bush long, long ago. Why? I never knew.

Was it the twenty-year age difference between their little black brother and his large, young, white wife? Could it be he was adopted? Hm? Will somebody say something? None of them spoke to me. I don't know why. They just nodded, feigned toothy smiles in my general direction and, after their fifteen minute showing, went home.

I never knew, or even recollect hearing, the names of my grandparents on my li'l black dad's side of the family. He was 40 when I came to be. Seeing as he was the youngest of at least three brothers, this would have put his parents in their seventies. This didn't strike me as ancient, heading in the right direction maybe, but not necessarily decrepit and or dead.

If they were out there I never knew where.

They had to have made a point of staying away, just as my mom and dad made a point of never mentioning them. I often thought if anybody knew what caused this dissension, this rift in the family bush, they of all people would. But they hardly spoke of relatives and when they did my mother spoke in code. "See where Bullet Head and Mushmouth have been married ten years."

"Well good for them," my l'il black dad would say. "Send 'em a, (belch), from me."

"Dick, this is your brother and his wife."

"Oh, well here, put a, (belch), stamp on it."

And, that was about it. At least I knew relatives existed, despite not knowing any of them.

Kids at school talked about having aunts and uncles and cousins galore and most of them even had two sets of grandparents. A lot of them even had enough relatives to have family reunions.

One night before the accident, I was lying on the floor alongside the TV with a bent wire coat hanger and a piece of aluminum foil, manipulating the rabbit ears every which way in a futile attempt at reception, so my mother and sisters could watch Lassie.

I asked if we could have a family reunion.

My mother stared at me then called my dad who was in the kitchen making his lunch for work the next day. "Dick, he wants to have a family reunion."

"All right," he said, stepping into the living room and just standing there looking down at me.

My mother and sisters stared at me also. Nobody said a word. I looked at each of them looking back at me in silence. I started to get nervous. The rabbit ears shook and I lost Lassie.

Then my dad turned away. "We'll have to do this again real soon," he said. They laughed hysterically. "And we don't call it a reunion, boy," he yelled from the kitchen. "We call it a run-in."

I laughed too, but not at the same thing they were laughing at. In fact, I didn't know what they were laughing at, or why I was laughing for that matter.

I did make one last earnest, yet feeble try, at flushing out the family bush.

Because I had never met or heard of any sisters on my li'l black dad's side, did not mean they didn't exist. Not wanting to chance upsetting him, you never know, I inquired one time about the possibility to my mother.

"Sisters? Why? Who wants to know? You? No, he doesn't have any!

Drop it!"

End of issue.

Just months before my dad's run-in with Rudolph, my uncle and grandfather, my mother's older brother and father, died.

My uncle was leaving a bar after a night of drinking. While backing out of his parking space, he passes out, floors the gas pedal, and plows into a snow bank, plugging up the tailpipe with snow.

The authorities blamed it on carbon monoxide poisoning. My mother blamed it on the alcohol. My dad simply said, "He had huge feet. Whattya expect?" Whatever that meant.

When my uncle died, his widow vanished with the kids. We never heard from them again.

My mother said my grandfather died from smoking cigarettes. He was ninety-two.

"Cigarettes my arse," my l'il black dad chimed in. "He was friggen old!"

The bush had dwindled to a fern.

At least my Uncle Jay, my mother's younger brother and last sibling, was alive and well and living, well, we never knew where he was living from one week to the next. He was a rather secretive, nomadic, yet colorful person. I only saw him when I was visiting my grandparents and he happened to be there, which was not very often because my grandfather preferred he stay away. This was not a difficult request for my Uncle Jay to honor, being he was a regular guest of the state prison system.

Grandma Millie, recent widow, my mother's mother, was a slight, winsome woman with a wonderful sense of humor. "Married from the day I was born to that man," she'd say.

She asked the driver of the hearse, if, once we arrived at the cemetery gates, she could drive the final yards to my grandfather's gravesite.

"Why's that, ma'am?"

"He often said one day I'd drive him to his grave. It just seems like the right thing to do."

"No."

Grandma Millie had a knack for attracting and entertaining people, telling nasty jokes in her cute, harmless way. "Then Dorothy said, ""So, Toto, what would you do with a pecker if you had one?"""

My grandfather had always been there for her. With his passing, after the last shovelful of dirt was thrown onto his coffin, she found herself unprepared to live all alone.

"No problem," my mother said. "You'll come live with the kids and me."

"Oh, I don't know." Grandma Millie was not one for decision-making.

"And I won't take no for an answer!"

"I'll just be in the way."

"Whose way? We have the room."

"Well, if you're sure I won't be putting anybody out."

"Don't be silly. Who would you be putting out?"

"What about--?"

"The girls will move to the bunk-bed room. You and I will share the big bedroom. It'll be fine."

"What about--?"

"Board? We'll talk about that later."

"Okay, but—"

"Work? We'll find you a job."

"Good. Okay, but where are you going to put--?"

"In the hall."

"But, it's a hall."

"Put a stove in a room you have a kitchen. Put a sofa in a room you have a living room. Put his bed in the hall he has his own bedroom. It's perfectly good wide open space going to waste."

"It's wide open because there's no door. He won't have any privacy."

"Well, I can't very well hang a door in thin air."

"Maybe we could build a wall."

"And when turkeys have wings they'll fly! It's my house. You are not living alone. Now, that's it! If he needs privacy the bathroom's right there."

"Oh, I don't know."

"He'll be fine, he'll be just fine."

This rationale from a woman so upset birds weren't using her birdhouse, she had me raise it to help the birds see it better. It was not in a tree. It sat on top of a pole. In the middle of the yard. There

was nothing near it. Even a blind bird could see it. In the middle of the night. During a raging snowstorm.

But, so she decided, so it was done.

By sheer coincidence, the day I learned of the new sleeping arrangements was the same day my mother was called by the principal to come to school and take me home. It seems I was being argumentative (?) and disrespectful (?) to my fifth grade teacher and generally disruptive (?) in class.

I told the truth then as I tell it now.

I'd missed a day of school the week before, attending somebody's funeral, so I had to make-up an arithmetic test. I was given a desk in the back corner of the room.

While pondering a long division question, a bird, a real bird, smacked beak first into a section of window running half the height and full length of the wall. The live bird saw and was attracted to the stuffed bird perched on the window ledge.

The kamikaze nature of the bird startled me.

I watched as the bird smacked into it again then flew away. I saw it coming a third time, I tried to get the teacher's attention, but she was writing on the blackboard, her back to me.

The bird disappeared, then suddenly re-appeared out of the glare of the sun and made a direct hit at the windowpane. I watched it fly away, following its path as it flew directly towards the sun. The glare of the sun caught me just right, triggering a sneeze like I have never sneezed before.

Multi-projectiles, wet, sticky, yuck stuff in both color and shape, spewed from my nose and mouth. This happened so suddenly and with such force, I had no time to cover my face or grab my sleeve, let alone a Kleenex, or move the arithmetic test out of harm's way.

This had to be the most disgusting sight I had ever seen in my life!

I quickly, quietly, carefully folded up the test paper, wiping the desk clean with the back of the paper, and gingerly tossed it in the waste can.

I raised my hand, I know she saw me but she ignored me. Finally she said, "There will be no questions taken while the test is being given. Put your arm down and be quiet."

So, that's just what I did.

A half-hour later I was told time was up and to pass my paper forward. I looked down at my desk, shook my head, and, out of nervousness I guess, started laughing. Slowly, not knowing exactly why, the class started laughing also.

"Pass your paper forward," she demanded.

"I can't."

"You can't? Why can't you?"

"I threw it away."

"You threw it away? Why did you throw it away?"

"There was a bird."

"A bird? What bird?"

"Never mind."

"Never mind? Never mind, what?"

Is it me or am I talking to Little Miss Echo? "I sneezed on it."

"You sneezed on it?"

"Yes.

"Then threw it away?"

"Yes. No."

"No?"

"No, first I sneezed on it, then I wiped off the desk, then I threw it away."

I offered to take it out of the waste can so she might see for herself. She said it wouldn't be necessary, though not exactly in a pleasant tone. My oratory on booger disposal was met with mixed reviews. My peers were in hysterics as she escorted me to the principal's office. The classroom was a good distance from the office but I still heard their laughter as I stood, nose to wall, in the hall.

By the time my teacher finished telling her version of the story to the principal and my mother, she actually had them believing I had purposely blown my nose on the test paper, callously throwing it away.

Not a word was spoken on the ride home. Upon arrival I went straight upstairs, cutting across the unexpectedly cluttered hall, tripping over a varied array and multiple piles of curious items trying to get to my room, my mother right on my heels.

I had no sooner stepped one foot into my room when she yelled at me to, "Get out of your sisters' room!" I stepped further in and realized my little world was no longer mine. She grabbed my collar pulling me backwards into the hall.

"Until you start acting your age, until you stop embarrassing your father and me, you know how much this will upset him when I tell him, hasn't he been through enough? Until then, this, is your room! Now clean this mess up and don't come down until you're done!" And she went downstairs.

I glanced into the big bedroom and saw my Grandma Millie's stuff all moved in and set up. Then it hit me. With my li'l black dad unable to be here, there was only one male left in the immediate family bush, besides myself, and this was my eccentric, wandering Uncle Jay.

All females in the family bush that I was aware of, were now living under my year-round summer house roof. Even when my dog Patches had her puppies, she had five females.

The one male, the runt of the litter, died because he wasn't strong enough to fend for himself. The day the puppy died my Grandma

Millie was the one who told me, in fact, it was a male and all the others were females. I couldn't tell.

Then she explained the runt theory to me. I talked to her about how sometimes I felt the same way.

She listened, then looked away, trying hard not to laugh, but did anyway, then gave me a big hug and told me to go blow my nose. She was a sweet little lady.

One glance into the big bedroom explained everything.

This had nothing to do with what happened at school. Everything I owned lay scattered in the hall. Overwhelmed, I sat on a pile of Archie® comic books and thought, 'The timing was just convenient for her. This move would've happened anyway, with or without any kamikaze bird.'

This is when I decided, made up my mind right there and then, if she could twist and manipulate a simple sneeze into an excuse to upset me this much, to make me feel this guilty, then I will never, ever, I don't care if I burst, I will never break wind in front of her.

If a sneeze could cause this much trouble, I could only imagine.

So I decided, so it shall be.

Chapter 3

A Dog By Any Other Name

His days were filled with therapy. Exhausting, grueling, tedious, physical therapy.

In his entire life, my dad had never known anyone who would do anything without expecting something in return. Now people who just a few months ago did not exist in his world were genuinely concerned about him. Taking care of his every basic need. Helping him eat. Bathe. Dress. Relieve himself.

For the most part, as he adapted to his new home, life, and world, most of the changes I witnessed were admirable and inspiring. On the other hand, some of the changes were small, tedious, and slow in coming.

Having never known the pleasure of a sauna or whirlpool, he looked at them as personal rewards, twice a day, for enduring the rigors of therapy. Change affected every aspect of his being. Rudolph had literally put half of him out of commission for the rest of his life.

The changes were so subtle at first, I reasoned the meds the staff were giving him, every hour on the hour, were causing a skin reaction. Am I the only one seeing this? Nobody ever explained.

Will someone tell a kid what the heck is going on? Or are we now playing a form of hospital censorship?

Fine!

It took a while for me to fathom the sauna and whirlpools were the cause and effect.

When I was nine and a half, he was dark brown. At ten, he's brownish orange. At ten and a half he's orangey with a tinge of yellow. Eleven, he's a yellowish pink. When I was just about to turn twelve the man had just about turned white. The sauna and whirlpool had found my li'l Caucasian Dad. The only reminder of the past? Nicotine discoloration on the fingertips of his right hand.

No one explained. No one said a word. I thought the man was part chameleon! But, in the long run, no matter what shade, tone or color he may end up, even paisley, he'd always be my li'l black dad.

Lying there day after day after day, week after week, month in and month out, whether he came upon the idea himself or someone suggested it, I don't know, but he began reading.

Not just sports or daily news, but books. Books that did not have staples in the middle. Real hard cover tomes. With dust jackets. All words, no pictures. Books that made him think. Made him curious, confident. Creative, clever and witty.

Once he started his journey of self-discovery and began rising from the ashes, he never once turned back, not a single page.

"If you seek intelligent dialogue, surround yourself with intelligent people. If you seek the company of arseholes, surround yourself with knotty-pine."

Confucius he wasn't. Confused, that's debatable.

My dad took great pleasure in his little Pearls Of Wisdom.

"There's more to life than just living."

"Whattya mean, dad?"

"You can't run a race standing in place."

"What are you saying, dad?"

"Never play leapfrog with a unicorn."

"I wish you'd explain, dad."

"Wish in one hand, shit in the other."

"Excuse me?"

Of all his Pearls of Wisdom, this one I will never forget. Wish in one hand, shit in the other.

In all we do, in all which passes by us and we pass by, we wish for the best and settle for less. We like, we love, we wed. We divorce. Pleasure to pain. Wish in one hand, shit in the other.

I know he thought this was the first time I'd heard it, but I'd had time to mull this one over, having first heard it a couple of years back when I was seven, almost eight. I was at the right place at the right time to hear him say it to my mother at the end of a most traumatic day.

For the longest time, more than anything in the world, I wished for a puppy, my first puppy. Finally, after months of begging and pleading, and against my mother's adamant wishes, just days shy of my eighth birthday, my dad brought home a most mangy, ill-kept, flea ridden, full grown Poodle with one ear.

"What is it?" asked my younger sister.

"It's a puppy," said my dad.

"It's a beast!" said my older sister.

"It's a dog," said my dad.

"It's a monster!" exclaimed my mother.

"Here you go, boy. It's a puppy dog."

"Oh, just what I always wanted." What else was I supposed to say?

Come bedtime, I spread out an old tattered blanket on the bathroom floor for bedding. A fuzzy orange ball, about the size of a ping-pong ball, became my puppy dog's first toy. My tiny Cub Scout alarm clock, about the size of a quarter, which had the most monotonous, but comforting, tic-tic-tic, was set under the bedding to soothe and induce my puppy dog to slumber.

Into the wee hours he was all puppy. My li'l black dad joked at, 'ripping that phucken dog's voice box out its arsehole,' if I didn't keep him quiet. He was joking, I'm pretty sure.

I went back 'n forth to the bathroom, as my sisters wanted nothing to do with the "beast", whispering words of quiet good night to my new puppy dog, "His bark is worse than his bite." The irony of it all. Finally all was quiet, as if my puppy dog sensed pending doom.

Come morning, I was stirred by the moving of the bunks as my dad got up to go to work. I lie awake, but quiet in my top bunk, eyes closed. He took forever to go downstairs. I wished it were winter because without a normal heating system, after all this is a summer house we live in year-round, he would be ready to go before he even woke up.

Finally, he went downstairs.

I heard him wrestling to put his jacket on. The sharp click of the kitchen stove igniting. The many little "clicks and ticks" the stove gave off, as the cold metal gave way to the warmth of the 350

degree "bake" setting. The heating log had quit long ago. The bake setting was just enough to ward off the morning chill.

He let out a long sigh as he sat down on the bottom stair step waiting for his ride to work. I wondered why he never drove. I never knew why.

I heard the match head scratch across the striker, igniting. Quiet. Then in one smooth move, he would inhale, then exhale, *poof*, blowing out the flame.

Quiet.

The smoke wafted up to my room through the floor vent. I heard his exhales.

Quiet.

Then he coughed. Then burped. Then coughed, and belched, and burped, and hiccupped, and burped, and coughed, and farted. Then sighed.

Then silent.

Smokey haze filled my room. I sneezed.

"You think you can make a little more goddamn noise up there? People are trying to sleep!"

Tires ground the gravel. Rattle of his lunchbox handle. Metal jangle of the broken kitchen doorknob. Heavy-handed slam as he left. Thud of the car door. Motor roar as they sped off.

And then, calm.

I climbed down from my top bunk, tip-toed to the bathroom, quietly opened the bathroom door, to find my new puppy dog, buddy, pal, best friend, dead. Dead!

Bedding torn, alarm clock gone, orange fuzzy whispies clung to his lips. I screamed bloody murder!

Variations of, "I'm surprised the monster lasted this long." "Thank Christ for little favors!" "Shut-up or you'll be next," came from the big bedroom.

I ran downstairs, catching sight of taillights as they disappeared round the bend.

"Why? Because it's your dog, is why!" my mother said. So, because my mother and sisters squealed at the thought of using the bathroom with a dead carcass staring at them, I had to wrap the tattered blanket around my no name dead puppy and drag him to my bunk bed room.

My puppy lay dead in the bunk bed room all day. Usually my dad arrived home from work between five-thirty or six. On this day he didn't get home until seven-thirty. By then everyone on my dead-end street had heard of my dead puppy. My dog. My no name dead puppy dog.

Nobody seemed concerned, despite my questions of "How?" and "Why?" They just wanted the animal out of the house. My older sister saw me sitting in the bunk bed room all sad.

"Would you feel better if we said a poodle prayer?" she asked.

"Yes. Do you know one?"

"What are you, an idiot? Of course not!" she said, laughing, running downstairs.

When my dad came home he carried "No Name" out behind the old weathered shed in the back yard for burial. As the long shallow hole grew, so the number of vacationing summer neighborhood kids grew. Though the hole grew longer than deep, the more he dug, the larger the crowd, the closer they drew to the hole.

No one made a sound as he laid No Name to rest and began to fill in the hole. That day, most every kid there witnessed death, burial, and my li'l black dad for the very first time. They knew he lived somewhere on the street or in the woods, but few knew he lived in my house, even fewer knew he was my li'l black dad.

As he threw on the last shovel full of dirt, the crowd began to disperse.

Then, I swear, may God strike me dead, the most bizarre thing happened.

As he tamped and slammed, tamped and slammed at the mound of dirt to smooth it out, the sound, "BBRRRING—BBRRRING—BBRRRING," rang out!

No Name had swallowed my tiny Cub Scout alarm clock! The slamming of the shovel had set it off!

"BBRRRING—BBRRRING—BBRRRING."

Kids went running in every direction. Running for their lives! Screaming and tripping, pushing and shoving, falling and stepping on each other to get away! Arms and legs were flying everywhere!

"BBRRRING—BBRRRING—BBRRRING."

I didn't know whether to laugh or cry. For a moment, my li'l black dad didn't know what to do either. He looked at me, looked back at the mound, pursed his lips, shook his head, turned and began walking back to the house.

"BBRRRING—BBRRRING—BBRRRING."

And this is when my mother asked and this is when I heard it.

"Aren't you going to dig him up? Dick, I really wish you'd dig him up."

"Is 'at so, Edna? Well, wish in one hand, shit in the other."

And he just kept on walking.

Chapter 4

The Ballad of J. Dean Presley

Uncle Jay, my mother's younger brother, was self-tattooed. The words "love" and "hate" cruelly administered, crudely lettered in blue ink on the backs of the four fingers of each hand.

He had the James Dean, unloved, unwanted, always brooding, uncomfortable to be around type personality down to the letter.

A white-T with a pack of Camels® rolled in the sleeve, dungaree vest, blue jeans, and well-worn, slope-heeled cowboy boots rounded out his daily attire.

The donning of a white, button-down cotton shirt, black leather vest and black spit-shined, pointy-toed cowboy boots meant he and his eye-catching girlfriend, Ronnie, or Veronica, kissed, made up, and were together, yet again.

A dirty blonde, naturally curled, twisted lock of hair dove from his hairline, hanging like a cliff-diver frozen in mid-leap over his forehead, always dead center perfect. Some days a pencil thin moustache, always crooked, never permanent. Add the perfect Elvis sneer, posed Presley posture, a wave of Old Spice: Voila. Warning. Do Not Touch.

He was husky, not large like my mother, his sister. A natural intimidator with a flash powder temper, he roamed the nightlife. He liked his liquor and was not one to back down from anybody in a bar fight. His scars, especially the two small facial scars he sported, attested to his nature.

The whole family regarded him as no more than an oft-jailed, loud-mouthed, out of control drunken bully with no job, no prospects, and no redeeming qualities.

I thought he was a pretty good guy.

When my grandfather was alive, for most school vacations and week-ends, I'd be schlepped to the city to stay at my grandparent's apartment to keep my grandfather company. He was a good ol' guy, already pushing seventy when I was born. He slept a lot. About the only thing I can say about him is he was a very good sleeper.

By fate, dumb luck, or mutual understanding, just like my folks, there was a twenty year age difference between him and Grandma Millie. I always thought this too much of a coincidence. As if done by design. I don't know. Odd at best.

On occasion after my grandfather had gone to bed, out of thin air, like a spirit in the night, Uncle Jay would appear and visit with Grandma Millie.

She'd greet him, snoring away in her recliner. Once awake, she'd pop her teeth in, turn off the TV, and make him something to eat. They'd talk awhile, drop a tear or two. Uncle Jay would promise to change his life. She'd give him a few dollars, turn on the TV, drop her teeth in the glass, and recline back to sleep.

Uncle Jay would then roust me out of bed and whisk me away in the middle of the night to Boston's seedier watering holes. This happened so often I had to wonder if he was tipped off to my visits by Grandma Millie, because this was the only way he could safely share time with me and not risk family confrontation.

To him, at one in the morning, the hour wasn't late. "The sidewalks are just rolling out. The night is just beginning," he'd say.

Knowing I would not be allowed in any of the bars, he would lock me in his old, but meticulously kept, pearl white, pin-striped,

Studebaker Golden Hawk, leaving me with a pack of Camels®, a couple of cans of Bud®, and the warning: "Do not unlock the car for anyone!"

In an hour or two he'd reappear with his black friends and we'd end up at one of their apartments, eating chicken, tossing shots, and singing gospel songs. Well, I ate and played with the dog.

"This is my favorite nephew," he'd say, grabbing my skinny bag of bones up in a rib-crunching bear hug. Fact is, I was his only nephew.

Just before sun-up he'd race back to my grandparents' apartment and drop me off with the warning: "Don't say a thing to anyone!" No one was ever the wiser.

I never knew from one time to the next when I would see him again.

Long ago, Uncle Jay was labeled the "black sheep" of the family. I never saw this side of him. I didn't even know what it meant. To me it sounded like he and my li'l black dad should have gotten along famously. But, he forbade Uncle Jay from stepping foot in the Great White Elephant.

My mother once referred to her younger brother as an enigma; my li'l black dad corrected this to an enema. And, in one rare but memorable attempt at defending her brother, she told him he had the wrong "impression" of Uncle Jay.

"Impressions are a lot like an arsehole relative," he said with a grin. "Everybody's got one, that one's yours." Nipped that conversation right in the bud.

Uncle Jay wasn't an idiot. He knew how the family felt about him and he had no problem turning the tables back on them with the words, the drama, all mentally rehearsed for weeks in a booze soaked haze.

"I live my life unmasked, unlike all of you, who live each day

worried your masks will crack and everyone will see you for the phonies you really are!"

After an outburst he'd be shunned and banned anew, until the next forgive and forget party.

Uncle Jay was never less then kind to me and as generous as an uncle could be to a nephew, that is if cigarettes and beer are good choices for a pre-teen relative.

Now with my dad institutionally incognito and no male relatives willing to come out of hiding or rise from the grave, one excuse is as good as another, then my Uncle Jay was all I had left.

I was not looking for perfection, just a bit of attention, a word of communication, some appreciation, an occasional visitation, a speck of consideration, willing participation, personal identification, an hour of individualization. Even if this person came with a history of intoxication, phuck it, I'll take it, so be it.

During one of Uncle Jays six months to a year RSVP stints, with time off for good behavior, my mother loaded Grandma Millie, my sisters and me into the overstated Rambler family wagon. We looked like any other typical American family out on a sunny Sunday drive or on a family picnic. We looked like a family with values, real values, like the Cleavers.

Off we drove to the Shirley Minimum Security Prison of Massachusetts to visit with my incarcerated Uncle Jay. Whatever my mother's intention, whatever life-lesson this was to teach us, was immediately thwarted when we entered the grounds and I spotted the sign: Shirley State Prison For Women.

"Well, this should be interesting," I mused, a bit too loud.

"What did you just say?" my mother asked.

"Nothing."

"Keep it that way! Eyes open, mouths shut! One word, you stay

50

here!"

We signed in, emptied our pockets inside out, and were led to a large, brightly lit, multi-tabled dayroom. The area made even brighter by pastel blue and yellow concrete walls.

The room was full with other visitors and "guests" of the Commonwealth of Massachusetts with everyone talking, arguing, crying or forgiving. Replete with little hugs, quick feels, and sneaky kisses, when the matrons weren't looking.

All conversations were held in hushed mumbles.

"Sounds like the Murmur Tabernacle Choir," Grandma Millie said. We laughed. I wasn't sure what was so amusing, but if Grandma Millie said it, it must be funny.

We sat waiting for Uncle Jay to be brought out. 'For a women's prison, there are a lot of guys wearing prisoner uniforms walking around,' I thought.

A surely combustible cloud of Old Spice preceded his entrance as Uncle Jay swaggered in. Wearing his best half-smile-half-sneer, he looked like a fox amongst the chickens. The one question never be answered because it would never be asked, "How'd you manage this?"

I'd seen my Uncle Jay empty a room before but this was a record.

"How are they treating you?" asked Grandma Millie.

"How's the food?" asked my younger sister.

"Did you get fatter?" asked my older sister.

"How's Veronica?" asked my mother.

"Phuck, Ronnie!" Uncle Jay snapped, looking away from her.

"Okay, girls, who has to pee?" my mother abruptly asked, ushering

my sisters and Grandma Millie up and out to the hall. Just like that, we were all alone.

"You know why she brought you here?"

"I think so," I muttered.

"What? Yeah? I'm your bad example."

"It's okay."

"You married yet?"

"Um-m, I just was eleven."

"Oh, you just was? Got a girlfriend? Want one? Hey, Sandy, c'mere."

A cute, petite, short-haired red-head came to our table. "Hey Jay, what's say?"

"This is my nephew. He needs a girlfriend."

"For how long?" They laughed. "Whatcha got in mind, handsome?" I smiled and fidgeted. "Oo-o, a shy guy. I like 'em shy. I like 'em shy between my thi—"

"Hey, Sandy, Jesus! What're you doin'? Kid's got virgin ears."

"You come back February fifth, year after next, in exactly twenty-one months, six days; Sandy'll fix your ear problem. Later, 'gater."

"She's a good kid. So, how's the battle goin'? How's your dad?"

"Sick, good."

"Well, is he sick or is he good?"

"Okay."

"Somethin' on your mind?"

"What're you doing here?"

"Six months to a year."

"No, why're you here?"

"Drunk and disorderly."

"No, this?"

"What this?"

"This is a women's place."

"No shit. Oh-h, phu..., didn't anybody..., I volunteered! I didn't kill anybody, dum-dum. This is minimum security. They're minimum security. I'm minimum security. You think they pay people to shovel snow? Think the women are gonna shovel? You think they unload the trucks and shit? Look around. Does it look like the visitors are visiting just women? This is easy time. Good time. I get my own room. Time goes by quick. What'd your mother tell you? Nothin' right? She's not here as the good sister, ya know that don't you? She moved Ma in, right? I won't see Ma again. Not alone. You watch."

"She'll let you visit."

"Maybe."

"Yeh."

"Oh, look what I got for you. I cut this out. I want you to do this."

"Charles Atlas? I already tried this."

"You're kidding? Well, this time put a stamp on it."

It cost a dime, right? Yeah, it's the same one. I filled out the coupon, taped a dime on it, put it in an envelope, and left it on top of the refrigerator to be mailed. Somebody took it and opened it."

"How do you know it wasn't mailed? You don't know. Maybe it got lost in the mail. Happens everyday."

"See, right here, it says, 'Picture your face on top of these massive shoulders!' Somebody cut out my school picture, pasted it over the face and left it on my bed. Kept my dime, too."

"Well, I can't say that happens everyday. What'd your mother say? Or did you even tell her?"

"Yeah."

"Well, what?"

"Promise you won't say nothin'?"

"Promise you won't ask me again?"

"Yeah," I said with a smile. "She said, 'What'd I expect for a dime?'"

"That was all? Did she tell you she did it?"

"No. I don't know who did it. I think I kn--"

"It was her, wasn't it?"

"Doesn't matter."

"You can't let people step on you. Speak up!"

"I know. I do."

"You don't. I can see it in your eyes, your face. You have to speak up."

"Why's she have to be so mean all the time?"

"There you go. There you go. There's a start. It's not you, you're just there. If it wasn't you, it'd be somebody else. And, listen, I'll tell you something. Patty may be older than you, but she's not getting out of this easy, either."

"She doesn't even talk to me."

"I know, ain't nothing new. Nobody talks to anybody."

"We do."

"We're cool, don't ya think?"

"Yeh."

We sat for what seemed the longest time with goofy, easy smiles. It could have been half an hour, more like half a minute, but a slow, comfortable, 30 seconds.

"Ronnie sent me a lucky rabbit's foot," he said, breaking the silence.

"That's nice."

"I threw it away."

"Why?"

"Cause there's a three-legged bunny hoppin' round somewhere out there. How lucky you think that bunny-rabbit feels hoppin' round on three legs?" He sat there with a deadpan look. It took a few seconds to sink in.

"You made that up." I was laughing. "Didn't you? You did. You made that up, right?" He finally broke and he was laughing. "Sh-h, here they come. Remember, you promised. The coupon, the dime."

"Stop saying that. Keep the dime. You call me. I'll be out soon.

I'll fix everything when I get out. Okay? Alright? Deal?"

"Deal."

"What are you two shaking hands over?" my mother asked, eyeing us with curiosity. "Making a deal in here is like shaking hands with the devil himself."

"Whattya mean by that?" Uncle Jay sneered, instantly angry.

"What? I was joking for Christ sakes!"

"So, what's the joke? I don't get it," challenged Uncle Jay.

"None of your business. I was talking to him!"

"Why would you say that to him? Stop picking on him."

"What do you mean stop picking on him? I'll pick on him all I want. He's my son, not yours."

"Well, treat him like it!" Uncle Jay sneered, snapping back.

"Go wait in the car," she said to me. "Go wait in the car! Whose dime is that?"

"Mine," I said.

"Where'd you get it? Where did you get that dime?"

"From me. I gave it to him. Why?"

"Give it. Give it! Here. If he needs a dime, I've got his goddamn dime!"

"Yeah, that's the problem," Uncle Jay muttered, as he gestured a "good-bye, see ya" nod to me.

Chapter 5

Geraldine and Erwin

My mother and grandmother were inseparable.

They were re-bonding, rekindling the past. Laughing at the reversal of just who was providing, who was housing, who was caring for who, now.

Funny, ain't it?

Hair appointments were on Mondays. Lunch Tuesdays. Movie matinee Wednesdays. Shopping Thursdays. Bingo Fridays and Saturdays. And Sundays. Ironic how a death in one house can breathe life in another. Thanks Grampa.

In her mother, my mother gained a sudden cash flow, constant companion and roommate. At the same time, I found in Grandma Millie a daily smile, a friendly face, and buffer between me and the unannounced physical outbursts my mother did not want my Grandma Millie, or anyone else, to see.

Even though the glares and undisguised, wild-eyed leers picked up considerably, I could ignore them.

What I could not ignore though was the coincidence between my Grandma Millie moving in, and the sudden, constant, pungent

aroma of vinaigrette the Great White Elephant had taken on. What one had to do with the other was beyond me.

My two sisters were still going through their "we like every boy in the world but our cootie brother" phase. Actually, this started way before my li'l black dad's mishap and continued to be encouraged as normal and humorous by my mother. So this wasn't really a phase so much as an everyday nuisance.

My little life was worse than bleak.

Even worse it was the off season, so except for the nose-picking kid who lived a few houses down, who had the most disgusting habit of gnawing his fingernails down to the cuticles, then, with no fingernails left to hook with, went nose-fishing anyway and ate his catch. Well, except for him, no other kids near my age lived on the dead-end street.

The only time I had any of my school friends over to the house, literally in the house, was when I let them come in when I was home alone. Whenever my mother went out she'd tell me, or if she wasn't there when I got home from school she'd leave a note warning me, not to let any kids in the house.

"What if they need water?"

"They can use the hose."

"What if somebody needs to use the bathroom?"

"Go in the woods."

"What if somebody needs to call their house?"

"Not on my phone. Tell them to go home and talk."

"What if somebody has an accident, can they come in then?"

"Know what? Maybe it's better nobody came over. How 'bout that?"

"But--"

"What did I just say?"

"Then can--"

"You're cruising. Don't push it."

"No, I mean, then can I go over to--"

"When? Now? Aren't you going to see your father? He's expecting to see you, you know. He's looking forward to it. If that's not asking too much. Is it? Is that asking too much?

"No."

"It's not his fault he's in there, you know. You're being pretty selfish. Do you think he likes being in there? Do you? Do you think he likes lying there day after day? Do you? Well, do you?"

"No."

"I think you'd better go upstairs and think about it. Go! I don't want to look at you. And I wouldn't make any plans if I was you."

"But it's vacation!"

"I don't give a good sweet shit if it's the second coming of Christ! Get up there! And don't cry to your grandmother! She's tired of your bullshit, too!"

I didn't believe the part about my Grandma Millie for a second.

And as far as my li'l black dad went, did I think he liked being in the hospital? No.

Did I think he liked lying there day after day? No. Did I think he'd rather be home? In all honesty? No. He was being cared for, had more friends, more attention, than he ever had in his whole life. And he didn't have to listen to or put up with her whackiness.

59

Was living the life of a paraplegic, being laid up in the hospital for the rest of his life, a life at all? No. But next to this, it seemed the lesser of two evils.

I'd sit on my bedroom hall floor quietly rolling a rubber ball across the linoleum. The ball would always roll back to me because of the sag in middle of the Great White Elephant.

Both my dead-end street and my dead-end life were long in need of a blast of fresh air. A life altering, positive awakening, or a good swift kick in the pants. Either of them, it didn't matter, whichever came first.

I'd fantasize about some nice family moving into the Great Gray Monster, and they would be open to helping my mother handle her stress. They would have some kids. A couple of girls my sisters' age, a boy my age, and they would all be normal, and this would rub off on my family and make a difference.

Then overnight, like famine to feast, a whole lot more arrived in the vision of a badly bruised and battered Buick.

Erwin stood 6'6" and weighed about 140 pounds.

Geraldine was just under 5' and weighed about 180 pounds.

Standing back-to-back I was struck by how much they resembled a lower case b.

Judging from Erwin's bald pate and three inch snow line rimming lobe-to-lobe the base of his bullet shaped skull, and Geraldine's squat rotundness, coupled with the gray, greasy strands of a long lost Dutch cut, I thought of them as ageless, hapless, and loveless.

The paper-thin walls of their great, gray, year-round summer house held few secrets. As their closest neighbors we heard all and with every passing hour they shared just a little bit more.

"Geraldine, do I have any clean socks? Geraldine, do I have any

clean socks? Geraldine, do I have any cle—"

"How in the name of hell would I know if you have any goddamn clean socks? How? How?"

"I looked, there's none. I'm gonna be late for work!"

"So, look harder! If I looked I'd find your goddamn clean socks! So look, look!"

Geraldine's voice made napping babies cry out. Eagles take flight. And squirrels: (a) grab their nuts (b) run (c) hide.

Their glass jalousie front door rattled and slammed. The sound of Erwin ripping open the rusted tool shed door screeched like nails on a blackboard throughout the neighborhood.

Geraldine didn't follow. No need. She just held her ground in the kitchen, just stood in place and bellowed. "Do you think you'll find your goddamn clean socks out there? Do you? Well, do you?"

Erwin cranked over the battered Buick and sped away down the dusty dirt road. Geraldine barreled out her front door making a beeline for my house and her new confidant. In minutes the story was out as to just how resourceful a man Erwin was.

Seems Erwin took a can of black spray paint and, "Be damned if that lazy good for nothing husband of mine didn't go and spray paint his feet and ankles black!" raved Geraldine.

Having sworn her new friend to a vow of secret silence, Geraldine reveled in telling her tale. My mother, in turn, as Geraldine quickly found out and had come to expect, reveled in telling and retelling the tale.

She would grind it out, over and over, to anyone whose phone wasn't busy, whose car was in their driveway, or whoever was walking by. By noon the entire dead-end street, down one side and up the other, had heard. My mother claimed to hate gossip and gossipers.

"But, let's face it," she'd say. "What else can you do with it?"

Geraldine and Erwin had, as Geraldine referred to them, a brood of three. Charlotte, the oldest, aka Cha-Cha. Miriam, the middle, aka Mimi. And, Reggie, the youngest, aka Reggie. Their extended family included a menagerie of pets. Most memorable were Chico, a nasty, perverse spider monkey, and Lulu, a snippet of an excuse for a dog Geraldine toted everywhere, tucked safely away in an underarm skin fold.

The only time Lulu made a peep was when Geraldine set her down. Then Lulu, in a frenzied fit, would yip-yip-yip-yip-yip in total abandon like a badly wired, unopenable, unstoppable, smoke detector. Lulu's yips cut right through your flesh and sat embedded on your nerve endings like fish hooks, or tortured notes on distorted sheet music. Lulu's yipping would stop as quick as it started when Geraldine tucked her back in the exposed womb.

Cha-Cha was hands down Geraldine's pet. A busty, bleached blonde, Marilyn Monroe styled sex kitten, Cha-Cha constantly teased, but never pleased, all the boys in school and in the neighborhood. Geraldine was clearly humored, even encouraging of Cha-Cha's ability to frustrate the boys and make them drool. She lived for and came alive through her oldest daughter.

Mimi was certainly not ignored but did not possess any of the God given assets Cha-Cha flaunted. Mimi was friendly, with a warm smile and easy laugh, but she was much more comfortable in the background with my older sister, Patty.

Though close in age, living a stone's throw apart, Reggie and I were not allowed to chum around much.

Geraldine thought I was a bad example because my mother's stories of me always slanted so my mother was the victim. Her exaggerations way out-weighed the truth. "He's grounded for a week! He thinks it's a riot my hair got wrapped around the washing machine wringers!"

Not true.

Well, okay, I laughed, but, when she first told her story she told it while having coffee with three women from the old neighborhood and they all laughed. Even my mother. Even me. I was sitting right there. I saw them. I heard them. We all laughed together.

The next time she told the tale was to my li'l black dad as we sat at the supper table. My mistake was two-fold. First, thinking she was retelling her "hair in the wringer" story as a sure-fire, laughable encore. And second, laughing before she reached the end, thus stepping on her big finish.

On the other hand, Geraldine's tales of Reggie had to be bigger and badder than my mother's tales of me. "Then, he went and shot that nice neighbor boy with an arrow!"

Nope.

Well, yes, he did, but the three of us were taking turns with bows 'n arrows. The nose-picker strapped on one of the hard plastic shin guards Reggie wore when he played catcher for our Little League baseball team.

The nose-picker said the arrow couldn't penetrate the hard plastic of the shin guard.

Well, to make a long story short, it could and it did. The arrow cracked through the plastic, bounced back off the nose-pickers knee-cap, and stopped. Because of the way the arrow just stuck out from the shin guard, it really did look like it had penetrated the knee-cap, but it hadn't.

So by way of half-truths, exaggerations, and gratuitous swapping of "pity me" tales, our mothers effectively canceled us both out in terms of being mischievous, relatively normal, given the circumstances, boys.

Black sheep aren't born they're nurtured, like everything else.

Geraldine did not like or trust me. My mother neither liked nor trusted Reggie, referring to him because of his boyhood weight problem, behind closed doors of course, as "Willie-Lump-Lump." I can only imagine the sordid names Geraldine whispered of me.

The two women entertained each other this way. Which family is more bizarre and which member will be ridiculed today to prove it. Erwin and Reggie were Geraldine's members of choice. For my mother, I was the chosen one.

"Tag. You're it!"

I called their game for two, "One-Up."

There were no rules.

No one else ever played.

Chapter 6

The Goodies Incident

It had been almost a year since Geraldine, Erwin, and the brood, moved into the Great Gray Monster. And, a little over two years since my li'l black dad went into the hospital and Grandma Millie moved in.

The lunches, movies, shopping, and Bingo dates were eliminated almost entirely, though the hair appointments and vinaigrette smell remained intact.

I was almost eleven and my li'l black dad was orangey-pink.

And, by this time, we were just about out of newspapers, comic books, old school work, and incidental pieces of wooden furniture that could be broken up and sacrificed for heat to the recently acquired potbelly stove.

The old potbelly appeared in the living room like magic, all installed, one day after school. "With stacks and stacks of wood available for the burning right in the backyard, in the woods," my mother said.

At first I was told it would save money rather than using the gas stoves bake setting every day for heat. For much of that winter the old potbelly supplied all the heat and all the cooking needs the gas

stove no longer could provide, since in truth, the Gas Company had shut the gas off.

By spring I had a paper route, TV Guide route, and Grit route. I sold Cub Scout candy bars, magazine subscriptions, and tormented the neighborhood, along with other door-to-door salesmen, by selling them Burpee Flower and Garden seeds and by trying to sell them Cloverleaf Salve.

Grandma Millie, still spunky for her age, whatever it might be, worked in a wood finishing shop. During the pot-belly stove winter she was my hero. Bringing home bags and bags of wood to burn, which meant my trips to the woods to forage for kindling was minimal.

Her job at the wood shop was sanding wooden plugs, or buttons. These buttons fit in the holes drilled into the furniture, to cover the heads of the screws.

She called the plugs "bungs" and they were inserted in the "bung-holes". She was amused by the word.

"Bunghole."

When she said it, you had to laugh, just the way it came out of her. She made it sound dirty in a funny way. Even when she used it in place of your name, "Get over here and give your Grandma Millie a big hug, you little bunghole." "Hey, bunghole, scratch my back." "Whith one auf you bunghoes hid my teef?" it was still funny. Maybe because she got a kick out of saying it.

"Bunghole."

My mother thought it was funny only when my mother said it. Funny, this was the only time it wasn't.

Erwin worked two full-time jobs, pizza cook and custodian, supporting Geraldine and the brood.

Neither Geraldine nor my mother worked. Divan divas the pair of them. One was always sick, the other always tired. The tired one

would coddle the sick one back to recovery road, then it was the other ones turn.

You got sick and tired pretty quick hearing them talk about being sick and tired all the time. My mother self-diagnosed her near daily bouts of fatigue, blaming it on a mystery ailment. (see: hypochondria) She was in bed for a week. Go figure.

Whatever Geraldine thought of me didn't really matter. I knew the game she and my mother played, pitting Reggie and me against one another. I figured as long as I knew the truth to the stories my mother was telling about me, this was all that mattered. And despite Geraldine's belittling stories about Erwin, I thought the man was a survivor, a very funny survivor, but a survivor.

On one particular morning, Geraldine would prove once and for all how low she would stoop in slamming Erwin, and how her rules of "One-Up" knew no limits.

The telephone rang. I jumped up from the breakfast table on the first ring.

"I'll get it. I said I'll get it! Sit down, finish your breakfast," my mother said in her stern, flat voice.

I went back to my seat and runny eggs.

"Hello? Good mornin' yourself, Ger," she said in her cheery, friendly voice. "Hold on. Sit down and eat your breakfast!" I looked up and scowled my, 'What are you talking about? I am!' scowl, as yoke dripped from my fork, to my chin, to my lap. "And don't you give me any of your looks," she said into the phone. "And clean up your goddamn mess!"

Which, by amazing coincidence, is just what I was doing. But, Geraldine couldn't see, you see. Geraldine didn't know.

"He's cruisin'! Whatcha say, Ger? Sure, sure, c'mon up, the kettle's on...hold on, hold on Ger. Will you go! Go! Just go! Go outside, upstairs, I don't care, just go!"

I would've put my unfinished breakfast in the sink and gone outdoors but she stood between the sink, the door, and me. Going up to my hall bedroom was the safer of the two choices.

"I don't know what I'm gonna do with...you get back here and put those in the sink! What the hell do you think this is? Yeh, c'mon up, Ger."

I gathered my plate, fork, and glass, slowly, and when the coast was clear, when she moved from the middle of the kitchen to hang up the phone, moving quick, I put the items in the sink and went outdoors. I felt like I'd slid into second avoiding the tag. Safe!

"Get up to your room!"

Yer out! It would do no good to protest the call, I went in, avoided the tag, and went to my hall.

Geraldine had invited herself up for tea and goodies. She'd bring the goodies.

Living a stone's throw from each other, I knew something was up when I heard the slam of Geraldine's jalousie front door, seconds after my mother had hung up the phone. From my hall window I spied her short, rotund form, as she lumbered up the dirt road.

She wore a formerly white, sleeveless, way too open, way too low-necked, way too much cleavage showing summer smock, all peckered over with wee multi-colored flowers. The constant ebb and flow of viewable flesh, the wavy, rippling exposed skin, along with the thought of unexposed tonnage, made me glad I had not finished breakfast. Her gait was all hers. She'd lean forward and let the laws of dynamics and gravity take over. She plodded on up the dusty road. A woman on a mission. Airy clouds of talcum road dust poofed up with her every earth-jarring step.

I nonchalantly went downstairs, taking my seat at the table. I could for a moment forget what I had just seen from my hall window, if it meant "goodies" were to be had. My mother stood at the kitchen

sink, washing the breakfast dishes, ignoring my presence.

"Yoo-hoo, Edna?" In her pudgy hand, her sweaty grip, Geraldine grasped an old, wrinkled, waxy, doughnut bag. Judging from the hang-weight of the "goodie bag," my guess was coffee rolls or Bavarian cream.

I glanced up from the bag just as Geraldine's beady eyes, and my mother's suspicious eyes, met. The thought of them as friends, neighbors, yet fiercely formidable foes in their day-to-day insecure lives, coupled with their game of "One-Up" was understood by me even then. They were both loopy!

However, what Geraldine was about to do was so nasty, it would push the boundaries of good taste to such an extent, the boundaries would forever more, no longer be.

Geraldine immediately dismissed me from my kitchen in a word: "Go!" I really hated when she did that.

My mother glared her patented, move or die glare. As I made my exit, I asked for a goodie, again I was struck by the glare. Then struck.

Only imbeciles, idiots, and fools hang around for more.

I went upstairs and snuck into my old room, taking up position over the vent the floor shared with the kitchen ceiling. I knelt above them, directly over their heads and the kitchen table, peering down.

Geraldine up-ended the goodie bag.

A "cruller" plopped out, landing with a thud, followed by a rolling dough-ball.

My mother caught the dough-ball just before it rolled off and dropped it back on the table.

Neither woman moved an inch or said a word, they just stood, staring at the goodies.

Cruller above the dough-ball.

From my vantage point, positioned on the table the way they were, it looked like a cartoonist's exclamation point.

It didn't occur to me then at such a young age, but for the first time in my life I was stunned and appalled. Yet, I managed to hold down a stomach full of disgust, along with gales of explosive laughter when Geraldine explained to my mother, "Erwin, that goddamn lazy, sneaky, no good, worthless, goddamn sad excuse for a husband," was incapable of making a trip to the john one night, so he did the unthinkable. Done, he pushed his single bed back in place, over it.

Judging from the petrified "nonpareils" sprinkled over both, I'd say the "goodies" were anywhere from six weeks to six months old.

If anything good came out of Geraldine's visit, it had to be I was forever cured of finding harmless ogres under my bed.

Chapter 7

Home, Sweat Home

It's one thing when a member of your immediate family passes away. At best awkward, when they are no longer near, when they're out there somewhere, just no longer available to you.

But life goes on in either case. You just wish they were within earshot to talk to when things go awry.

I rode with my mother to visit my li'l black dad often. But, not being able to talk with him privately, to keep him abreast of the daily foolishness and folly, he may just as well have been a million miles away.

Within days of school ending and the long-awaited, much anticipated beginning of summer vacation, my mother had a vision. She decreed the sagging, white-shingled, red-trimmed, two-story, over-sized, year-round summer house with two sitting porches front and back, would become a sagging, maroon-shingled, white-trimmed, two-story, over-sized, year-round summer house with two sitting porches front and back, this summer.

The paintable surface of this pauper's palace would add up to three stories, including the eaves.

It was also decreed this task would be a most notable endeavor for a kid my age to undertake. Not to mention the hundreds, hell, coupla thousand dollars to be saved on contractors' fees.

My opinion never asked, my vote never cast.

"Do I have to paint the eaves, too?" I asked, lugging paint into place.

"Do you wash your ass when you take a shower?" my mother replied.

I would have said, "I think I would if I had a shower," but I liked the way my teeth naturally aligned.

I approached the enormity of this literal white elephant in three phases.

Phase 1 - Standing ground level, paint around the entire dwelling as high as I could reach. When the sagging middle was factored in this would take care of row 14 entirely, most of row 15, some of row 16, and a little of row 17.

This would also take care of the month of June.

About seventy, aged, multi-layered, New England white, paint-sucking and cracked, wooden-shingled, wavy rows, enveloped the palatial palace. Eaves be damned. If I make it that high, I'll paint 'em with my phucken eyebrows!

Phase 2 – would usher in the ladder. The wooden ladder. The old wooden ladder. The old wooden shaky ladder. The old wooden shaky ladder with dry rot to be precise.

"Can't we get some staging?" was my weak plea.

"You wanna break your goddamn neck?" she snapped.

I bit my tongue and thought, 'Yeah, you're right, my mistake. I am so much safer twenty feet in the air, under a ninety-five degree sun,

gingerly poised on the old wooden shaky ladder with dry rot, juggling brushes, rags, scrapers, cans of paint, and much needed Orange Crush. Why must I always be so demanding?'

"There's a right way, a wrong way, the only way, and my way," my mother would say, to my annoyance, to Geraldine's amusement. "Do it my way and you wouldn't be making this even harder than it has to be. Leave the soda on the ground."

She had borrowed the old wooden shaky ladder with dry rot from Erwin. He had every intention of letting me use his new, lightweight, extendable, aluminum ladder, for my summer's task, but Geraldine, in her infinite wisdom, explained to my mother how it would be an "absolute sin, a goddamn shame" to let the new, lightweight, extendable, aluminum ladder, become maroon-spotted and smeared before they had a chance to break it in.

I had reached midway between the first and second story, and warily, oh, so carefully, climbed down the old shaky wooden ladder with dry rot, just as Geraldine had finished telling my mother her soul-searching decision.

Hot, sweaty, maroon scarred from head to foot, out of Crush, with my guard down, my mouth opened, and I heard a voice I recognized as my own say, "What the phuck did I do to deserve this?"

It must've been the way it came out. With just the right amount of verve. Punched up in just the right spot. Crude but articulate. I looked at both women with my best, 'What was that? What? Did you say something? I didn't hear anything. Did you hear anything? I didn't say anything!' look, with no luck.

They heard. They both heard. I could tell by the way they stared at me, mouths agape, slack-jawed with nothing coming out. Their mouths were always open with food going in or gossip coming out, but this time neither woman had a word in their head or a pork rind in hand. A dead give away they'd heard. They were speechless. I used the moment of silence to ponder, quietly, the calm before the storm. 'There'll be hell to pay for that one. It's just a matter of

when and where.'

Well, I'll be damned. It's here and now.

"I don't know," my mother said, "maybe the same fucking thing you did to deserve this!" as she pummeled, wailed, gouged, bit, and kneed me onto the back porch, into the house.

Geraldine just disappeared, just left and went home. I pictured her grinning as she went.

Now that this has been "explained" to me, I clearly see why summer in New England is the best time for a kid my age to be out in a ninety-five degree sun, lugging the old shaky wooden ladder with dry rot around like a crucifix! How could I be so blind?

Phase 3 – would finally introduce Erwin's spanking new, lightweight aluminum extension ladder, if only because the painting of the eaves had to be done to unite the eaves with the old blue roof.

Blue. Blue Roof. Old Blue Roof. The Old Blue Roof.

My acquisition of the now questionable "new" ladder had more to do with loss of interest by Geraldine and Erwin's brood as a hand-over-hand jungle gym, laid horizontal, either end placed on the roofs of Erwin's old shit boxes; a rot-infested Renault, and a devastated DeSoto, than the obvious fact: I really did need it!

Weeks of Willie-Lump-Lump, the nose-picker, and the rest of them monkey-swinging on the new lightweight, extendable, aluminum ladder, had buckled and warped it so much, getting the extension to extend was a daily symphony of banging and slamming with a hammer on my part.

Becoming intimate with each and every one of the old, weather-beaten, formerly white, now newly-coated maroon, paint-sucking, wooden shingles, was to soon become a three-month exercise in futility and thanklessness.

As the maroon wave rose up and up and up, leaving the old, dull, weary, weathered white awash in its wake, as roof and eave lines grew closer and closer and closer, as I slathered paint over the last of those cracked, separated, aged, off-white, buck-toothed slats, what would've been obvious to a blind monk who never bothered looking up, suddenly became quite clear to my mother.

"I simply cannot live in a three story maroon house with a blue roof! Why didn't you tell me?"

This sight never bothered me.

However, to suggest I could repaint the next summer did.

But what really bothered me was Geraldine claiming I owed her one hundred and fifty-five dollars to replace the ladder I had obviously (?) ruined.

"Tell my mother to deduct it from what she's paying me. Alright?"

She said this would be fine. I also thought this would be fine. In fact, doubly fine. A fine lie, because no money was ever mentioned, and, a fine time to enjoy some of the nine days left in my summer vacation, so, I ran away.

With really no place to run, I returned an hour later.

My mother asked if, in fact, I said this to Geraldine. Expecting some part of me to get battered, bruised, or broken, I dug my heels in, braced, and swallowed hard.

"Uh-huh," I said.

"Well, what a coincidence. I was going to pay you one hundred fifty dollars for the paint job, but seeing as you told Geraldine to collect from me, I gave it to her."

"So, everything's okay then?" I asked warily, knowing full well no money was meant for me, or paid to Geraldine, or would it ever be.

"Except for the five dollars you owe me, it's okay with me. Okay with you?"

"Uh-huh, okay."

There was a brief silence as she stood staring at me. I stared at her hands hanging at her side, expecting any unexpected move. None came. She turned and went into the kitchen. The screen door slammed as she went outside. I stood there for a moment. On one hand I was relieved, of course. On the other, I was geared to make a dash upstairs in case she had a change of heart and came busting back in.

I stood in a long breathless silence. Waiting. It was over.

I went to my hall thinking about my near miss. I had lied, got caught, disappeared for an hour, yet nothing about me was battered, bruised or broken, and it only cost me five bucks. All in all, I thought I was having a pretty good day.

No sooner had I laid on my bed then I heard the kitchen screen door slam. I bolted upright, my heart jumped. Then, quiet. I listened with all the intensity I could muster. The second stair creaked as it always did when stepped on. Why is she creeping upstairs? She usually charged up stomping like a wild rhino. My imagination raced with what was coming and what would happen.

The fifth rubber stair tread slapped back down on the bare wood step, as it always did when it slipped free of the climber's heel. The growing shadow of the skulking figure loomed larger and larger until finally, "Your mother said you owe her five dollars, she needed it, so I gave it to her," Grandma Millie said. "You owe me five bucks, bunghole."

"Really?" I exhaled.

She went to her room to drop her bags and remove her coat. "Why did you owe her five dollars?" Grandma Millie asked, crossing my hall to get to the bathroom.

"I don't," I whispered. "But now I owe you."

Even though we were on the second floor, and even though I saw my mother through my hall window sitting in a lawn chair out in the yard, I know how innocent conversations pass very clearly through these hollow, paper thin walls. I told her the story speaking softly through the crack where the door misaligned with the casing.

As I lay back down, Grandma Millie reappeared and sat on the edge of my bed. Quite unexpected she said, "Don't worry about the five dollars." She placed her hand on my forehead. "You're all hot and sweaty. Are you okay?" she asked.

"I don't know what to do."

She just shrugged and smiled. "I heard a cute story today."

"Tell me."

"Don't tell your mother."

"Okay."

"Once upon a time, an elephant was having lunch in the jungle."

"Um, is this going to help? With a moral or something?"

"I don't know, we'll see. Are you going to keep interrupting?"

"No."

"Once upon a time, an elephant was having lunch in the jungle. The usual, you know, nuts, berries, nothing special, balanced fiber. Along came a gnat, hops up, and lands smack dead center on the elephant's bum."

"Ouch," I slipped. "Sorry."

"Try as it may, try as it might, the elephant could not shake free of

the gnat. By an extreme stroke of good luck, Sammy Sparrow happened to be flying by. Seeing the elephant's pickle, Sammy zooms down and zaps the gnat dead!"

"Pickle," I laughed. "Pickle."

"The elephant was so taken by Sammy's mercy, friendship blossomed. ""I can't tell you how grateful I am," said the elephant, aka Grandma Millie in a very deep elephant voice. ""What's your name?"

Tucking her thumbs in her armpits, flapping her arms as if fluttering aloft, talking into an elephant's voluminous earflap, in a high-pitched tone, she said, "Sammy. Sammy Sparrow. What's yours?"

"Ellie. Ellie Phant. If I can ever do anything, anything at all to repay your kindness, you just holler."

"Anything?" Sammy asked, unsure and shy.

"Anything!" Ellie boomed.

"Well, I always wondered, I mean, I always wanted--," sputtered Sammy, as he flitted about nervously.

"What? What is it little buddy?"

"Well, you're a female elephant, right?"

"Say no more my little friend, you just saddle on up!"

"If you don't stop giggling I'll stop right now," said Grandma Millie.

"Sorry, but when you do Sammy your arms flap funny."

In an alarming high tone she said, "Gee, thanks!"

"Welcome," I laughed.

"That was Sammy thanking Ellie. Pay attention."

"Oh."

"Sammy took his position and proceeded." Grandma Millie's arms flapped furiously. "nee nee nee nee nee nee nee!" Then, in mid-flap, she stopped. "That's how sparrows do it, you know," she said, and began flapping as furious as before. "nee nee nee nee nee nee nee nee!"

"All the while, perched high overhead, a monkey had been watching with sheer enjoyment. Excited, the monkey swung on the branch knocking a coconut free. The coconut slammed down on Ellie's head! Ellie let go a deep, resounding, RRRROOOOAAAARRRRR!"

Unaware of the coconut, Sammy, 'nee nee nee nee nee,' paused, peered about to Ellie and said, "Oo, I'm sorry, nee nee nee, am I hurting you?"

I laughed myself silly at Grandma Millie's elephant, bird and monkey act.

"Is there a reason you told me this story?" I asked.

"Yes. To hear you laugh, bunghole."

To this day that was the best story I ever heard.

Chapter 8

Me Tarzan - You Vain

All the men in the family bush were unknown, unavailable, missing or dead.

I couldn't talk to my li'l black dad about anything for fear of upsetting him. Not like I wouldn't have chanced speaking to him, but my moments alone with him were scarce and short. So he was unavailable. It really didn't matter. My problems seemed small compared to his and, for what it was worth, at least I could run away from mine.

Uncle Jay was the one missing. We hadn't heard from him in a year or more. I thought about him a lot and, though he could take care of himself, I did worry about him a little.

He was the only one left in the family bush who could pop in at anytime and see for himself what was going on. He was the only one who could help me put this whole mess into perspective.

I felt my life was in a downward spiral and no one cared. It wasn't enough I was out of control, I had to open my mouth to prove it.

"...don't forget men, the 3-Rs. You can push through life without them, but life is going to push you back a little harder. You'll push again and again and, life is going to push you again and again and,

life always wins, unless you're up to the challenge.

Only the foolhardy charge into combat, step through the ropes, throw their hats into the squared circle of life with no game plan. The 3-Rs men, this is the foundation, the building blocks of your game plan. The seeds, the very seeds you need to…"

Coach was on a roll saving student's souls.

Like a Marine drill sergeant, his voice boomed through the double doors I stood the other side of, peering through the doors dividing slit. I was late for gym. Coach hated late and me. No, not really. I just wasn't Coach's rah-rah athletic type. I tried out, but never did play school ball. Truth be told, closest I ever came to playing ball was when I got jock itch.

I gripped the doors handle, pulling ever so careful, ever so quiet, and peered in. My gym mates sat in a semi-circle listening as coach chewed up and spat out life's little secrets. Judging by his red-faced glow, I had missed a good sermon.

3-Rs? Have my dad's fingers been on the pulse of the puzzle which escaped humanity for so long? Could it be rage, reach, and random reason, in fact, held the answers to life's little secrets? Could it be my li'l black dad's a li'l black wizard?

So many questions. So few answers. So little time. And even fewer people to ask.

Coach stood stiff, rigid, seemingly inflexible. His sparkling white Keds®, perfect fit gray sweat pants, shiny blue wind-breaker zipped halfway, a crisp white Polo shirt underneath, collar snapped taut, rigid jaw, piercing blue eyes, stern face, and shiny jock-head crew-cut, made him look like he just stepped from the centerfold of "Coach of the Month."

The only thing missing was the whistle which usually hung from around his neck. Now it hung on my hall room wall. I didn't steal it. I'm no thief. I found it the day we had gym out on the football field. I was just holding it, just to make sure it was his before I

gave it to him. I still wasn't positive it belonged to him. Maybe he was just forgetting to bring his whistle from his perfect home. I only found it a month ago. I think it best I hold on to it a little while longer, just to make sure.

Now, if I could just sneak, slink, or slither in before he took attendance, I stood a very good chance getting away with yet another late arrival.

I wanted to scream, "Turn around!" He did. I damn near died.

I made my move. Smooth, quiet, like vapor, not even breathing. Quick and low, with sure-footed conviction. Twelve more, eight more, five more, one more step, and I'm sitting with my mates.

"You're late!" Coach boomed, turning as I squatted. He stood at parade rest, clutching the attendance clipboard behind him. "The 3-R's are?"

"Rage, reach, and random reason?" I muttered to the kid near me. The kid rolled his eyes. Well excuse me, you unenlightened little rich shit.

"On your feet!" Coach barked.

"I'm not sure," I said, standing.

"You're not sure?"

"Yes. No. I mean, I don't know."

"You knew ten seconds ago!"

"No I didn't."

"You a funny boy, Funny Boy?" I looked away, shaking my head, no. "Think you'll find the answer over there clown? Think one of your buddies will tell you, Funny Boy? They're laughing at you, not with you! Get it? The 3-R's? Entertain us!"

"I didn't, I--"

"That's not funny! Who thinks that's funny? No One? Make me laugh, Clown Boy! Give it your best shot! The 3R's are?"

"Rubbers. Ribbed or Regular."

C'mon Coach, let it go. You can do it. You wanna laugh. I can see it. Let it out. Laugh goddamn you! I wish the floor would open up and one of us, preferably Coach, would disappear.

My skinny legs trembled. I wished I had long pants on. 'You'd be grateful for what you have on, if you had no pants at all,' I heard my li'l black Confucius say.

Or, at the very least, I wished I'd worn any other pair of socks than these brown, sheer, just-above-the-ankle ones. 'To the boy with no socks, you are envied.'

Or, at the very, very least, I wished I had on a pair of Keds®, not these ratty Hush Puppies®. 'A pair of Hush Puppies® will take you further than no Hush Puppies®.'

I just wished I owned a pair of Keds®. 'Wish in one hand, shit in the other.'

I wished at the very, very, very least, I had proper gym shorts. Not these crotch clutching, gold lamé trunks I wore per my mother's orders, Geraldine was so generous to offer in place of my long lost gym shorts. They looked like a guy's bathing suit, but they fit so tight and were gold in color. Smooth, shiny, gold lamé. I had never seen anything like them. And nobody else would either.

I let my gym shirt hang loose, hoping to hide the embarrassment, then it looked like I had nothing on underneath. Some days you just cannot win.

"Okay, Funny Boy, up the rope!" Coach barked.

Despite past attempts, I never made it up the ropes, and I feel an

84

attempt now is not going to end any different. 'Leave me alone!' I yelled, silently.

"Climb, Funny Boy! That's an order!"

"Coach, I don't have--"

He barreled through the class, stopping just short of my first facial hair. He poked at my chest. Spittle flew everywhere.

"Do not call me Coach! Never call me Coach! You will never be on any team of mine! Got it, Funny Boy? I am your Phys Ed teacher, that's it! That is all I will ever be to you! You would never make the cut on my team! Got it? Do you understand?" I nodded. "I can't hear you!"

"Yes."

"Yes, what?"

"What?"

Why won't he just die? This is not going to have a happy end, I just know it. Now I wished I'd skipped gym like I had planned in the first place. The only reason I changed my mind and came at all is so I could take a shower. Look at me. My nerves are shot, my self-esteem is Swiss, and now he wants me to call him, 'Sir?' I'm sorry but I just don't see it.

"Yes, what, Funny Boy?"

"I don't, what--?" I stammered, confused, but adamant.

"Get up that f'ing rope, Funny Boy!"

Well, seeing as he put it that way, I, uh-oh, "No, no sneakers."

"You offend me. You disrupt my class and you come unprepared? Get up or get out of here! Get up there or get out!"

Remember Tarzan ropes hanging, suspended from an I-beam?

The idea: make it to the top of the rope, sign your name to the I-beam, and you are Jock-Man or some damn thing.

So, I'm at the rope, pen between my teeth. With a hop and a twist, hand over hand, up the rope I go. Maybe it was an adrenaline rush from the way Coach had spoken to me, or a sugar rush from this morning's double dip into the sugar bowl which I added to my already Sugar Sweetened Sugar Smacks®, whatever, I don't know, but, by some Divine Miracle I made it to the top of the rope, ratty Hush Puppies® and all. Thank-you very much, I am Jock-Man. Yes!

Now I'm at the top of the rope, staring at the I-beam, at all the names of all the successful Tarzan climbers before me. I really didn't care who'd made it up here before me, there were only two places to look and I was not about to look down.

Holding on for dear life with one hand, I took the pen from my mouth with the other, and I started to write my name. FFFF-RRR-AA--

"What the--?" Coach chortled. "Are you wearing gold lame?"

I froze. In mind's eye I clearly saw a cartoon character, plummeting from a cliff, wearing gold lamé. I took the vision for what it was, an omen.

"DON'T YOU LET GO, FUNNY BOY!"

I knew I was going down.

"DON'T YOU LET GO!"

Many last words ran through my mind. 'Oh, we're not laughing now, are we? Now you wanna help? Now, now you wanna lead me? Hold on for the team?' But all I heard come out was, "UP YOUR AS..s..sshhhhhhh....!"

In desperation, I slapped my hand atop the beam, leaving the pen behind. Then clutching at, gripping to, squeezing that rope like a lifeline to Hell, down I went! Burnt flesh, human sacrifice, trailed the rope above me!

My butt slammed to the mat! My face smashed to my knees! My teeth mashed into my lips! My head crashed back to the floor! Dazed and bleeding I lie there, gazing straight up.

It's over, right? Wrong!

Remember the pen? The pen is now descending on me at about 177,000 miles per hour! It was a Paper-Mate®. This is way before they came out with the Bic Banana®. That pen weighed at least 15 pounds.

It bore straight down on me like an arrow with eyes! Impaled!

To this day I am the only person in Tarzan rope climbing history to get ink poisoning of the right nipple!

Chapter 9

The Fabulous Beulah

My little life was so heavy I felt my very shadow was a burden.

As a kid, being poor won't kill your spirit; you will hardly notice. Not having an abundance of relatives and friends will not kill your spirit; you can dismiss what is not there. Not receiving a daily dose, a steady, dependable daily dose of love and consideration will not kill your spirit either, though it will harden it.

What will take its toll on any human soul, especially a kid, is a lack of humor. Where there's a smile, laughter lurks. Where there is laughter, love follows close behind.

I was suspicious of people I should have trusted, lied to by those I had no choice but to trust, and angry at, and with, everybody.

There's a very good chance even I wouldn't have helped me.

I was on very shaky ground. My spiral allowed to continue for the amusement of others, or so I thought. Met by loud glances and silent tsk-tsk's by everybody who could have spoken up. Any teacher, any townie, any official, anybody in any "fix-it" position.

Any, any, any. ANY!

One late fall afternoon, walking home from school up my dead-end street, past the deserted summer cottages, images of the owners filed by. One by one, I saw each of them walking past in mind's eye. I saw them in memory as I clung for dear life, two, three stories up, all summer long, as I did my paint and juggle act.

I often wondered why not one of them questioned why I was being treated as nothing more than slave labor? At the very least, why didn't one of them stop and say, "Nice job, kid." Or, "We're having a cook-out, c'mon over." Or, "Here, have a soda." But, no one ever did. Oh, they were looking, I know they were looking, but they were never looking when I looked to them.

Over the years, especially the summers when my dead-end street was crawling with life, I know some of these people saw fragments of beatings commence in the yard, then were quickly ushered inside. I knew living in an un-insulated cavernous shell they heard the yelling, screaming, the anguished cries.

"Stop! Stop! I'll Be Good! I'm Sorry! Please, Please, Please! Don't Throw, Don't Kick, Don't Punch, Don't Bite, Don't Gouge, Don't Dig, Don't Twist, Don't Bend, Don't Pull, Don't Scratch! Don't, Don't, Don't, Don't, Don't! Stop, Please, Stop!"

But, they chose to do, to say, nothing.

Then again, why should they? This was their three-month fantasy of success. Flee the inner city tensions, the heat, the smog, for three months of lakeside lounging.

If no one person is directly responsible for creating a given problem, then it becomes so very easy to ignore. "It's none of our business. Besides, he probably deserves it. Whattya expect? He's the kid who looked at me funny last summer. Don't get involved. What problem? What's wrong with house painting? He's learning a trade. You missed a spot. What doesn't kill you will make you stronger. Nice lawn."

So I picked up a stone and threw it through a cottage window. It felt good. So I did it again, and again, and again, and…throughout that entire fall and winter, whenever the coast was clear, those

90

windows were my release.

With every rock, every shatter of glass, I felt the frustration lift from my shoulders. In reality, I knew what was happening to me was not their fault, but what was happening wasn't mine either. In the spirit of caring, have a rock.

Here it was Friday. My week-end plans? See Monday. Pathetic.

It never failed. Just when life stank unbearably, sniff. Old Spice! From out of nowhere my Uncle Jay came running up behind me, grabbed me up by my ears and ran me for a dozen or so steps on the tips of my Hush Puppies down my dead-end street.

"Put him down!" my mother yelled, spying from some window.

He finally let go, just as I felt my ears were about to be ripped from my head. He laughed uproariously. It was good to see him, to hear his laugh. I was just glad I could hear. Painfully glad. Period.

"How'd you get here?" I asked, gently touching my ears, not so much to comfort the pain, more to take inventory.

"Ronnie dropped me off. She'll be back to pick us up."

"Us?"

"Yeh. You like wrestling?"

"Wrestling? You mean wrestling, wrestling?"

"Don't hurt yourself. Yeah, wrestling, wrestling. Wanna go?"

"You, me and Ronnie? Nobody else?" Suddenly I found myself energized, grinning at the thought of a night away. An entire night of fun with my two best friends. Beautiful Ronnie and Uncle Jay, my favorite people.

"Why you got a date? It is Friday night. I hoped you'd be free, but if you got some hot stuff hidden away I can always ask your

sister."

"No! Yes! I mean, when? Now? Let's go."

"As soon as Ronnie gets back."

"Did you ask?"

"You're clear. See, I told you I'd take care of things. Didn't I?"

"That was almost two years ago."

"Quit yer bitchin'. My watch is slow."

"Wow, this is going to be so cool! Who's wrestling? Kowalski? Gomez? The Animal? The Chief? Do you know? Who?"

"Me."

"No, really?"

"No. Really!"

I did not doubt for one second Uncle Jay was telling the truth. Sorta.

I couldn't fault him for his cocky bravado, even if it was false, not only about this wrestling venture but all the other attempts to make himself look bigger than life. This was the way he wanted to be seen by the world, especially his family, Ronnie, and me. Daring, adventurous, willing to take it all on. It's just most of his tales would eventually prove to be unfounded, half true, or blatant lies. So? At least no one ended up getting hurt or looking the fool, except Uncle Jay.

I ran in the house. The wooden screen porch door slammed, bouncing off the frame its usual three, slam, slam, slams.

"Hold the door. Don't slam it!" yelled my mother from the living room.

"It's kinda late now," I muttered, crossing the kitchen, entering the living room.

"What?"

"I'm going to the wrestling," I happily announced.

"Is that what you were told?" my mother said, eyes affixed on her favorite soap opera, The Secret Storm.

"Yeah."

"Did I say you were going?" she said, her eyes still glued to her soap.

"Um, I thought—"

"You thought?" I had her attention. "You know what thought did don'tcha? He shit himself and thought someone else did it," she said, followed as always with the look of a learned philosopher.

She thought this line was clever and used it whenever the opportunity presented itself. The only time I thought this line was funny was when I was five or six and I ate too much black licorice before bedtime.

As I slept, it went through me like water. So quiet, so unexpected the intrusion on my system, when I awoke I really could not believe I had done this. At that young age, I was baffled.

"Me? I dunno. I thought someone else did it."

Then she tried to make the line work.

"You thought? You know what thought did don'tcha? He sh...," she stopped, suddenly silent. A confused of total bewilderment came over her as she struggled to figure out where her infallible lifelong joke went wrong.

From out of the blue, from somewhere, some darkened corner, some hidden crevice, somewhere in the house, my dad chimed in, "A little redundant there, don'tcha think, Edna?"

She got real upset, stomping into the bedroom, slamming the door behind her. For a long time I thought redundant was the worse name you could call anyone.

Grandma Millie and Uncle Jay laughed at my mother's line. Because it was funny? No. But, if you wanted the night to happen, laugh, play the game.

Mine was a nervous laugh. Let her think it's funny, keep her humored til you're down the road. Play the game. It's knowing how to play the game.

Ronnie drove up in the Studebaker. I ran up to my hall, threw my school books on the bed and grabbed my whistle. At wrestling all noise is welcome. I ran back downstairs. I glanced out the window and saw Uncle Jay and Ronnie waiting in the car, laughing. I remember thinking they were, oddly enough, the perfect couple. I hurried to the door saying my good-byes.

"Don't go yet. C'mere," said my mother.

"What?" 'Lecture time,' I thought.

Walking into the living room, I felt lightheaded, dizzy.

"Whattya mean, what? I want you to know I'm not crazy about this."

I stood, appearing to be listening, but I had a reeling feeling.

"I'm only letting you go because Ronnie's going."

Something smelled terrible.

"She'll keep an eye on you."

I thought I was going to pass out.

"I don't want to hear any stories."

Turning to run out, I figured it out.

"I'm not through yet."

Old Spice and vinaigrette don't mix!

"You just stay near Ronnie!"

Gladly. Ronnie just smells like Ronnie.

I dove in the backseat. Off we went.

"Where we headed?" I asked.

"First we gotta drop Ronnie off," said Uncle Jay. "She's working tonight."

"But I, oh, I get it." They laughed at the lie Uncle Jay told my mother about Ronnie going to the wrestling matches with us.

Ronnie and Uncle Jay couldn't be any different. She was quiet and reserved, yet, your friend from first hello. Pretty. Long dark hair, dark eyes, and blessed with perfect, blemish free, natural skin tone.

"Ats'a my Italiano," said Uncle Jay, as Ronnie popped open a Bud, then another, and another, passing them around. "My leettle piece'a pepperoni pizza pie." We laughed at his attempted accent. "And I don't want you bummin' smokes from me all night either," he said, glancing at me in the rearview. "So here. Smoke 'em while you got 'em." He tossed back a pack of Camels®.

The intent was right. The lie was wrong. The timing was perfect. Cool.

He pushed back, driving with one outstretched arm. Ronnie leaned back on him, nestling under his right arm, draping his arm across

her chest. I had a dribble of Bud on my chin, a soggy Camel in my mouth, and a smile tattooed on my face. Uncle Jay cranked up the volume and supplied the bass as Ronnie sang to the tunes blaring from the radio. WMEX-AM. Arnie "WOO-WOO" Ginsberg.

"He's a rebel and he never, ever, does what he should,
And just because he doesn't do what everybody else does,
That's no reason why we can't share love."

'I'm going to the wrestling matches!' I yelled in silence.

We drove to Ronnie's house to drop her off. A volley of goodnight kisses followed. Well, Ronnie kissed. I thought Uncle Jay was gonna eat her lips off.

How could anybody not like this guy? Why did everybody treat him like he was a throw away? He was fun, funny, exciting, not afraid to try anything, not afraid to fail at everything. But, so what? Uncle Jay lived by the words of James Dean: "Live fast, die young, and leave a good looking corpse!"

He was so taken by this Hollywood cliché, he took a string of little white pom-pom fringe balls and with a black marker wrote a letter on each pom-pom ball, snipping off the pom-poms that fell as spaces between the words and strung them up in the Studebaker.

I couldn't imagine him old. I couldn't imagine him young. I couldn't imagine him dead. As infrequent as his visits may have been, I couldn't imagine him not in my world. Most of all, I couldn't imagine what he did to end up atop the family's hated list. So, as we drove, as we drank and smoked and the radio blared, I asked.

"It's a gift," he said with a hearty laugh.

"Whattya mean?" I shouted over the blaring radio.

"I'm the baby."

"So?"

"You know when your mother grabs her side and makes her pained face and says, 'It's gas,' like you care or really give a phu...?"

"Yeah."

"Well, I got news for ya, little nephew. It ain't gas. It's me! She's thinking about me. I'm the thorn in her side."

"The thorn?"

"What?"

"What thorn?" I yelled over the music.

"Your mother's eleven years older than me. She'd catch my beatings for stuff I did. Gramps and Grandma Millie figured those things wouldn't have happened if your mother was keeping an eye on me. She caught so many beatings I should have gotten, she thought I couldn't do anything right." He stared off, smiling. "And, Gramps and Millie? Well, they thought I could do no wrong. Then your mother would catch her own beatings, she was no angel ya know, then she'd bring her beatings down on me. It was like a vicious circle."

"Sounds like a three-ring circus."

"What?"

"Sounds like a three—" I started to yell as he turned down the radio.

"Close, damn close."

"She'll listen to the neighbors, everybody else, never to us, never to me."

"I know. Your mother brought a lot of this on by herself. I don't know what her problem is. Unhappy, depressed, whatever. Don't get me wrong. I think it's a shame what happened to your father,

but there's no good reason why she can't get something together. She's not setting a good example or doing herself any favors being this sour and angry all the time."

"Sometimes I don't know what to do."

"Just be yourself, kid. Be true to yourself."

"What about you?"

"Sometimes I think about you kids and about a family. Then I look at your mother and think, 'Nope, ain't gonna happen.' Hey, I ain't no prize, but if any of them think I'm changin' now they got another think coming. I've done and gotten away with more than they'll ever do or imagine. Before it's too late, I wanna get away with a little bit more."

That pretty much sums up the conversation on the ride there. And, for the first time in a long time, somebody I loved and trusted was talking with me and life made sense.

Thanks, Budweiser®.

We sat outside the Armory.

Wrestling fans were still streaming in though I heard the occasional sound of a cheering crowd coming from inside. Uncle Jay finished the opened beers.

"I think we're late."

"We're okay," he said with a belch.

I read the sidewalk sandwich board. "The Masked Maniac, Crusher, Tasmanian Tarzan, Golden Boy. And in the featured match, putting her Woman's East Coast Heavyweight Title Belt on the line, from parts known only to the unknown, the one, the only, The Fabulous Beulah!"

"Um, Fabulous Beulah? I thought it was Fabulous Moolah?"

"Pretty close though," he laughed. "Maybe they're sisters."
"I don't think so."

"Did they get my name right?"

"Did you change it to Beulah?"

"No."

"It's not there."

Walking into the Armory, I couldn't tell, I really couldn't tell one way or another whether this wrestling story was real or not. But just in case something about this was true, I couldn't say to him what I wanted. 'It didn't matter. It's good just having you around'. I didn't want to sound mushy but he was all I had, relative wise. It just didn't matter. If it were true, I'd be doubting him just like everybody did. If it weren't true, I'd be putting him on the spot for an explanation.

As we approached the ticket booth I heard people yelling and screaming through the double-hung doors. I wondered why we were paying to get in if he's wrestl..?

"Work through the crowd and wait by the doors," Uncle Jay said.

He spoke to a big guy standing in front of a "No Admittance" door. "Never heard of you," I heard the big guy say. This was not a good sign.

The big guy opened the door, stepped in, stepped out, stepped back, and a huge, big headed bald guy, wearing a shiny red cape and shiny black tights, appeared in the doorway. From the photos out front I knew it was Mr. Crusher. This was a good sign.

Uncle Jay was doing all the talking, explaining something. Mr. Crusher just shrugged his shoulders. This was not a good sign. Then, like a dawning, Mr. Crusher let out a very loud, "OH-H-H-H!" He spoke to the big guy, nodded at Uncle Jay, pointed to me,

and said, "Enjoy the show." And the big guy escorted us into the hall. This was a very good sign.

"Didn't know," said the big guy, and he left us.

"Didn't know what?" I asked.

"Where do you wanna sit?" Uncle Jay asked. I shrugged. "Looks like a couple of seats up in the back there. Go ahead. I'll be right back."

Looking back over my shoulder I saw Uncle Jay slip through a curtained doorway manned by two burly heavyweights, each wearing striped referee shirts.

I made my way through the crowd, stepping on a minimum of toes, and found the last two seats that were together. Looking down at the wrestling ring, I realized how smoky it was. Billows and billows. 'This has to be unhealthy,' I thought, as I pulled out my smokes. An older kid sitting near me looked at my smokes so I offered him one. As he took it, some guy, his father, uncle, I dunno, cuffed him upside his head.

"You want a hole in your throat to go with the hole in your head?" he said, crumbling the cigarette, throwing it to the floor. "Those things'll kill you," the man said to me.

'And a few more cracks upside his head won't?' I thought, looking away.

The place was packed. Two, three hundred people. Kids were running up to the ring, slamming their hands down on the mat.

Posters and black and white headshots of wrestlers and boxers, then and now, were tacked up around the room. I recognized Killer Kowalski, Pepper Gomez, and Haystack Calhoun, from the wrestling show on TV Saturday mornings. They wouldn't be here tonight. I looked for my Uncle Jay's photo. Nope. Not a good sign. I smiled.

The match ended with some guy dressed in a Tarzan outfit the winner. The crowd applauded half-heartedly. Didn't miss much. The announcer took the mike, declared a winner, the Tasmanian Tarzan, the lights went up and he spoke about upcoming shows. All eyes were on the curtained entrance, waiting for the next brawlers.

'If Uncle Jay walks out from those curtains, I'll just die right here.'

A poster of New England's most noted boxer, World Champ Rocky Marciano, hung by the entrance. Marciano beat Jersey Joe Walcott for the Championship Title in '52. He retired in '56 with a 49-0 record.

I used to own an authentic pair of Rocky Marciano boxing gloves. I got them for Christmas a couple of years back. Well, they weren't really real. They were smaller than I expected, and hard, and stiff. The brown plastic outer covering made even stiffer because of the wintry cold Christmas morning.

Mine weren't the big leather kind like Willie-Lump-Lump and the nose-picker got for Christmas.

I knew I was walking into a short-end-of-the-stick moment when my mother hollered up to my hall, saying, "The boys are outside with their boxing gloves on. Why don't you go out and join them with yours?"

I grabbed my winter jacket, zipped up, pulled on my boots, laced up my boxing gloves with the aid of my teeth, pulling too hard on one plastic lacing, snapping it in two.

Damn.

I glanced out my hall window from the top of the stairs, watching the two of them tussling, sparring in the snow-packed dirt road running alongside my house. I noticed immediately, even from this distance, compared to mine, their gloves were enormous. And theirs didn't have a shiny brown plastic look like mine. And their laces flung about like long shoelaces, long, white shoelaces, not

101

tied in a rigid yellow bow like the one I could tie. A moment of doom was pending.

I went downstairs and stood at the window at the bottom of the stairs watching.

"Go, go out." said my mother, sitting with my sisters and Grandma Millie watching the Christmas festivities on TV.

"Oh, the Macy's parade," I was stalling.

"What, this the first time you saw the Macy's parade? Go out, they're waiting."

"Is he Fess Parker?"

"What's it say on the screen? Davy Crockett?" my older sister said.

"How many Davy Crlocketts do you know?" said my mother.

"He was Daniel Boone, too, though, wasn't he?"

"I don't know. Are you going out? Go out, go out!" my mother said, annoyed at my presence.

I pawed and spanked and jangled and clanked at the broken kitchen door knob in a half-hearted attempt at going outside. Much to my dismay the door opened. I stepped out into the snowed-in screened porch grabbing at the outer doorknob as best I could, slamming the door shut behind me.

"Don't slam the door!" I think I heard my mother say.

Startled, Willie-Lump-Lump and the nose-picker stopped sparring, eyeing me through the porch screening, standing there.

"How'dja make out? Did'ja get 'em?" Reggie asked.

Cha-Cha had tipped us off weeks earlier we were getting the gloves.

"Yeh. I'll be right with ya's."

I just couldn't do it. I pulled at the doorknob, pushed against the door, and went back into the living room.

"What now?" my mother said, rolling her eyes.

"Did you call me?" I asked.

"No."

"Oh. I thought I heard you call me."

"No."

"Oh, look. Lassie's in the parade."

"What do you want?"

"Nothing. I thought you called."

"No."

"Oh."

"What do you want?"

"Look, Trigger." I said, a sure fire conversation starter.

"So? Go, and don't slam the door."

"I put a letter on top of the fridge," I said, exiting the room of Christmas cheer. "I'm sending for something. Can you mail it tomorrow?"

"What am I, your maid? Leave it, I'll get it."

"I think maybe I can fix this doorknob for ya."

"What, right this minute?"

"Okay."

"Will you go outside? We're trying to watch the parade! What is the matter?"

'Oh, phuck it,' I thought. I couldn't tell her about the gloves without her taking it like I was ungrateful. Might as well get it over with. I went outside.

I shoved my yellow-laced, tied-in-a-bow, shiny brown plastic goober gloves under each arm, pushed open the screen porch door, ran over to my two friends and started bobbing around like they were. I pulled my mitts out from under my arms and wound up to take my first swing.

Willie-Lump-Lump and the nose-picker immediately stopped sparring to get a good look at the rather bizarre looking sissy mitts.

Unfortunately, I didn't think they'd want to inspect them so closely and I swung just as they stopped. I nailed poor Willie–Lu--, ah-h, Reggie, on his forehead, dropping him hard on his butt. He landed sitting upright, then, fell backwards. The nose-picker looked at me and scowled.

"What?" I said.

"Those things are like bricks."

"So's his head." I said, grasping my right-gloved hand. Reggie sat up shaking his head.

"You okay?" I asked. "I thought you were ready." He got up without saying a word. "Ready now?" They were done boxing.

Reggie asked to see my weapons of destruction. I held them out. They looked them over. The nose-picker pointed out the label, Authentic Ricky Marcano Boxing Gloves.

"Oh, they musta sent the wrong ones by mistake," I said.

They laughed and went off down the street, punching each other on the arm and boxing the air.

"See ya later, guys."

Heading back to the porch, I stopped and began sparring with a big old tree in the back yard. I barely tapped the tree and the cold plastic split. Out popped small ragged pieces of cloth. My now ruined Authentic Ricky Marcano Boxing Gloves were in fact factory stuffed with cloth remnants, bits and pieces of old dolls clothes.

"Good seats," said Uncle Jay, climbing into his seat from behind me.

"Yeah."

"You okay?"

"Yeah."

He sneered a crooked smile, making his pencil thin moustache seem even more lopsided than usual. He put me in a headlock and gave me a noogie on top of my head. I felt like everybody was watching. He let go, we laughed. Why does he think he has to impress me? I hated the thought he made up a tale for my benefit and I'm the one who is going to get the third degree about what didn't happen tonight when I get home.

"You'll like the next guy. He's a good friend of mine. Golden Boy Tad."

"Uh-huh."

"What?"

"Tad?" I had to chuckle.

"Our next combatants," said the announcer, "from the State of Maine. Maine, where even the moose wear plaid, let's hear it for the Masked Maniac."

A very large, very animated guy, dressed all in black, burst through the curtained entrance. He represented his wrestling name to a T, acting like a raving maniac. Even without the head mask this guy would scare the hell out of you. The crowd met him with a chorus of boos. The Masked Maniac growled right back. Some of the more daring audience members tried touching him as he rumbled to the ring. What thrill could anybody get telling their friends they touched the butt of some guy called the Masked Maniac?

"And his opponent, a crowd pleaser and lady teaser, get off your hands and give a rousing New England welcome to every girl's dream, every mother's son, direct from Miami Beach Florida, Golden Boy Tad."

'What kind of a name is Tad? Must be a Miami thing,' I grinned.

The two striped shirted guys, standing at the entrance, held the curtains aside and out stepped Golden Boy, the whitest looking guy I'd ever seen in my life. He had perfectly coifed golden hair and wore shiny gold trunks. Alarmingly similar shiny gold trunks. The memory chilled me.

He didn't have a single hair on his perfectly posed Adonis body. In his arms he cradled two bouquets of long stem gold roses. Golden Boy stood there. The crowd went nuts with approval.

This was definitely a Good Guy versus Bad Guy match.

People gave him a standing ovation. My Uncle Jay jumped up and gave out a long, shrill, fingers in the mouth whistle. I stood and applauded, too. The kid I gave the cigarette to just sat there, until the guy he was with gave him a crack up side his head. Again. Suddenly, the kid jumped up and started hooting.

Moving like a posturing pony, Golden Boy began strutting to the ring then stopped. Ladies shrieked. Husbands and boyfriends

applauded and laughed, and looked at their wives and dates with a wary eye, then back at Golden Boy with smiles of contempt.

The Masked Maniac beckoned, daring Golden Boy to climb in the ring. Putting both golden rose bouquets in one arm, he waved the Masked Maniac off with the flick of his wrist. The crowd howled with delight.

Golden Boy ascended the four steps to the ring apron and strutted around the outside of the ropes. He took a golden rose in his free hand, and every female in the house made a definite move, a demonstrative motion at getting seen, so Golden Boy would throw a rose to their area. Wherever a rose was tossed there was a moment of pushing, pulling, and shoving. A mini-melee, until someone held up the golden rose, victoriously.

My Uncle Jay even got caught up in the moment. He looked so big and goofy vying for Golden Boy's attention just like the women. Somehow, a rose sailed right in our direction. Uncle Jay, and the guy who cracked the kid up side the head, lunged, aggressively knocking and shouldering people out of their way.

They each had a hand on the gold rose, the other guy a bit firmer, until Uncle Jay gave the guy a solid elbow shot in the side and pulled the trophy away from the guy, who stood grimacing in defeat. The kid looked at me, he was smiling. What goes around comes around. Uncle Jay slid the rose down the front of his shirt for safekeeping.

Golden Boy leapt over the top rope and the Masked Maniac rushed him. Golden Boy raised his hands in a halting motion, stopping the Masked Maniac in his tracks. The referee, holding a hand towel and Avon type perfume bottle, went to Golden Boy, sprayed his hands and chest and toweled him dry. The Masked Maniac was beside himself, acting out his fury.

Finally, the bell sounded. The Masked Maniac rushed in again, grabbing Golden Boy and spinning him around, locking Golden Boy's arms skyward in a full-nelson. The Masked Maniac roared in victory. The roar gave way to a moan when Golden Boy

wriggled, a questionable wrestling tactic, free of the hold.

The Masked Maniac came at Golden Boy again and again and again with the same butt-wriggling end. Golden Boy strutted to the side of the ring where we were sitting and leaned over the top rope. The Armory was a frenzied madhouse.

Uncle Jay and I were caught up in the moment. He whistled his shrill whistle while I yelled and stomped like I had never done before. Ever. From across the ring the Masked Maniac broke into a full run at Golden Boy in the hope of knocking him ass-over-tea-kettle over the top rope onto the hard floor.

The crowd yelled their instructions to Golden Boy. "Turn around!" "He's coming!" "Watch out!"

And, at the last second, Golden Boy stepped aside and the Masked Maniac flew over the top rope, landing in a heap on the floor outside the ring. Uncle Jay bent down to me and, competing with the crowd, said, "I helped him get that move down!"

"Who?"

"Who d'ya think?"

"Golden Boy?"

"Of course, Golden Boy, knucklehead! You okay?"

"Yeah."

The match ended with the Masked Maniac being counted out, then carried out, on a stretcher. Golden Boy Tad circled the square ring, one last show of strutting and prancing, much to the largely trebled screams of the crowd. He left amidst squeals, handshakes, pats on the back, and autograph seekers.

"We'll take a short break and return with, Beulah!" said the referee.

"BEULAH!" the crowd mimicked loudly.

"Beulah!" he repeated.

"BEULAH!"

"Who-o-o?"

"Fabulous BE-U-LAHHHHHH!" Obviously a crowd favorite.

"We got here late. We missed a couple of matches," said Uncle Jay.

And there it was. His out. Now when I get home I simply say, "We were late and Uncle Jay missed his match." Perfect excuse. Who could deny him? No one. Perfect. I don't know what disappointed me more. The thought he lied to me or not seeing him climb in the ring. God knows he was big enough and tough enough to handle just about anybody. 'Oh, well, no harm done,' I thought. But, there had been. It'll be left unspoken, but there had been.

"Want to get some fresh air?"

"Nah."

"What's up? You're about as much fun as a hooker with a conscience."

"Nuthin'. I'm good."

"Alright then, I'll be back," he said, as he climbed over his seat and left.

I sat watching the crowd. There was a ruckus at the curtained entrance. Golden Boy had stepped back out with a handful of headshots. He gave half to each of the door guys. They sold while Golden Boy Tad signed his autograph.

I watched a very excited, very animated girl wearing a tight sweater and tight pants, talk to Golden Boy. Then in her dancing

excitement, she turned so her back was to me. I saw she had what appeared to be a bulging spinal column running from the back of her neck, down the middle of her back, split off in different directions at the base of her bum, and down to the cuff of each of her pant legs. My curiosity got the best of me. I decided to take a closer look.

I made my way through the smoky haze and milling crowd. I finally made it to the entrance and stood there, trying to look like I had a purpose in standing there, trying not to look too obvious while I stared at the girl's backside.

"I can sell you a photo," said one of the referees, laughing, "but I can't sell you that, kid."

"I don't give a fuck what you were told! Not back here you don't!" barked a voice from down the hall the curtains blocked from view.

Both striped-shirted referees and Golden Boy turned around, pulling open the curtains. A massive, well-dressed, bejeweled man was giving Uncle Jay hell. They walked towards the curtained doorway, right towards me. I couldn't let him see me, he'd know I had heard the outburst. I moved behind, found cover behind, the person closest to me.

It was the girl with the tight pants and sweater, the one with the outgrown spinal column running down her clothes. Now that I was this close, I saw even her hair was pinned back tight. A row of assorted size pins ran from the neck of her sweater all the way down to her pant cuffs. Pinned back so tight, from the front anyway, she looked curvaceous and alluring. From the back, she looked like a reptile. Somehow, without being told, I understood immediately. 'She's doing the best with what she has.' It bothered me I'd know this. And I knew it always would.

Uncle Jay emerged from the entrance in a huff and went to his left. I went right, making my way back to my seat. I pulled out my smokes, catching the kid who got cracked upside the head looking my way. I made a small motion to offer him one. Whoever the guy was with him caught me.

"Do it and I'll crumble all you have left," he said.

"Try it and this time you'll get an elbow to your head," I said.

Then, Uncle Jay stepped over the seat and sat next to me. "I meant speaking up for yourself at home, dum-dum," he said with a smile to me and a scowl to the guy who thought twice and sat back down.

The lights dimmed twice. The crowd scurried in all different directions to their seats. The announcer climbed in the ring with the mike. He stood ring center waiting, just waiting, then said, "Beulah."

"BEULAH!" parroted the crowd, but louder.

"Beulah," he repeated

"BEULAH!" came the cry back, even louder.

"Who-o-o?" prompted the announcer.

"Fabulous BE-U-LAHHH!" the crowd roared in unison, their favorite chorus.

And from the curtained entrance stepped the most enormous woman I have ever seen in my life! The crowd thundered with approval and laughter. To be honest I laughed, too. But, not out of disrespect. I laughed at the image of this immense black woman, Fabulous Beulah, and my li'l black dad in a clench.

His words came to mind, 'If I want any shit outta you, boy, I'll squeeze your head.' The thought lingered. Beulah could squeeze his head like a zit. Beulah would squash him, period. 'Come'n git yur li'l black dad pancakes!' I had to laugh.

My own private joke.

Fabulous Beulah trudged heavily toward the ring.

She looked neither happy or upset. In fact, she looked rather bored. Ho-hum, another payday.

She paused on every step, pulling herself up by the ring pole. The four ring poles seemed to give in, surrender, bow in, then fall back in place when she released.

On the first step up to the ring apron, much to the howl of the crowd and totally unexpected by me, Uncle Jay ducked his head down and let out a groan. On the second, he let out a longer, louder groan.

On the third, an even louder, longer groan. And on the fourth, and last of Beulah's pole bending, rope tightening, back breaking pulls, Uncle Jay let out a deep, dark, guttural rumbling, intensely building, powerful moan. As if on cue, three hundred people joined in to finish, with Uncle Jay orchestrating the ensemble in a most hideous, disembodied, monstrously loud, cavernous groan!

Fabulous Beulah made it to the ring apron and paused to catch her breath, it seemed. Just when I thought the crowd volume couldn't get any louder, Beulah bent over to climb between the ropes into the ring. Everybody hooted or howled, yelled or screamed, or let out a holler, whoop, or shriek. This couldn't get any more embarrassing.

"You forgot the popcorn but brought the wide screen, didn't ya?" Uncle Jay yelled.

I was wrong. This could get more embarrassing. The crowd roared with laughter. Beulah stared into the crowd looking for her tormentor, not amused.

"This match is a one fall, winner take all match for the Women's East Coast Heavyweight Title. The opponent for tonight's matc--," the announcer was called to ringside by a referee.

"What movie you showing? The Great Divide?" Uncle Jay shouted.

Beulah looked into the crowd with searching, piercing eyes. Not finding her irritant, she raised her middle finger in Uncle Jay's general direction.

"I'm sorry, ladies and gentlemen," said the announcer. "Fabulous Beulah's opponent is nowhere to be found."

"She ate 'em!" Uncle Jay shouted.

Beulah studied the crowd for her heckler.

"Ladies and Gentlemen," said the announcer, "we are prepared to give any woman, any daring soul one hundred dollars, if they can stay in the ring for three minutes with the Fabulous Beulah."

The crowd buzzed. Fabulous Beulah looked around. Uncle Jay stood up.

"That's not a shadow behind ya, that's your ass!" Uncle Jay was on a roll.

Beulah now had her tormenter in sight. She motioned Uncle Jay to come down into the ring. The crowd erupted. Uncle Jay waved Beulah off. He was standing, shuffling about in his excitement, his back to me. I had no choice but to stay seated so he wouldn't trample me. He was acting like I wasn't even there. I was positive he was drunk as a skunk!

"I'm sorry sir," said the announcer, "we're looking for a woman."

I guess I got a little too caught up in the moment, 'cause the next thing I know, peering out from behind Uncle Jay's butt, my twelve year old cracking alto hollered out, "Me too!" The crowd thought I was adorable. No, honestly, they did.

Uncle Jay looked down at me in disbelief. He set his hand on my shoulder and laughing, grabbed my arm, raising it and me up in

victory, then shoved me back down into my chair. Then, in an act of macho defiance, Uncle Jay turned back to face the ring, peeled off his vest, and tore his shirt open. The gold rose fell out. He caught it, draped it behind his ear, put his hands on his hips, and in a mocking fashion, swiveled his hips.

The announcer and Fabulous Beulah stared at Uncle Jay. I couldn't see him clearly from my angle, but knowing him as I do, he was doing something annoying and rebellious, like crossing his eyes and sticking his tongue out at them. Whatever it was he was doing, the crowd roared at his antics.

Then the announcer did a most curious thing. He scratched his upper lip.

Uncle Jay raised his hand to his face and flung something towards the ring. The announcer and Fabulous Beulah looked at one another and each gave a unanimous shrug.

"Fabulous Beulah accepts the challenge," said the announcer. "The dressing rooms are through those curtains."

The crowd was in a frenzy. Uncle Jay stepped over me, dropping his vest, and the golden rose as he passed. I glanced at his face and his moustache was missing. He made it to the curtained entrance in a hail of hoots, hollers, and slaps on the back, disappearing through the curtains. I was laughing and applauding.

Then it hit me. This was his wrestling match. He had this planned all along. The wearing and flinging of the fake moustache was all part of the show.

'Cheap theatrics,' I thought. But this was no tall tale. Now when I go home I can tell them this was the real thing. Uncle Jay actually climbed in the ring with another wrestler. Yeh, it was a woman, but not any woman. He climbed in the ring with the Women's East Coast Champion! The Fabulous Beulah! Cool!

"He's my uncle," I said to the kid and the slap happy guy with him.

"Your uncle? Really?"

"Yeah," I said laughing.

People sitting near nodded, laughed, and waved to me. One of his tales, finally, was the real thing. And I was the one to witness it. The sole witness? No. I have an Armory full of people to back me up.

One of the burly referees at the curtain gave the ring announcer a signal.

"Ladies and Gentlemen."

'Oh, my, God, I don't believe this.'

"For one hundred dollars."

'No longer—'

"One three minute round..."

'did I have to defend the guy—'

"of havoc..."

'simply because he was my uncle.'

"pandemonium..."

'Now I can say to anyone—'

"of unbridled mayhem..."

'who spoke wrong of him—'

"I give you the Women's East Coast Champion..."

'I was there!'

"The Fabulous BEUUUULAHHHHHH!"

'I was there!'

'And for the first time on any canvas..."

'You weren't!'

"in any ring..."

'I was the one—'

"anywhere..."

'I saw—'

"direct from beautiful downtown Brockton, Massachusetts..."

'with my own eyes—'

"let's hear it for, "The JAAAAY BIRD..."

'Uncle Jay's—'

"JUUUUDY MAC!"

'TITS!!!'

The Armory went berserk!

What I wanted to know first, 'Where in the name of hell did he get those?' Second, and just as important, he stood in the parted curtained entranceway wearing a one-piece black and white striped bathing suit. A woman's one-piece black and white striped bathing suit.

Question, 'Why is my Uncle Jay wearing a woman's one-piece black and white striped bathing suit?'

'Answer, Mr. Gullible, your uncle is really your aunt and has been

for twelve years. Twelve goes into twelve, um, carry the one, once. One whole lifetime. Yours! Your whole friggen life.'

'Nobody said a thing to me! If you're never told, whattya know?'

'Whoa. Not this time, Gullible Gus! This is one of those times when life is just a little too short to explain the obvious to a snot nosed kid.'

The crowd had been whipped into an insane frenzy. They were going nuts. We all saw what walked through those curtains; we all saw what walked out.

'Wow, he'll do anything for a laugh,' I thought.

As Uncle Jay broke and ran to the ring, I couldn't help but wonder how much money he was getting paid to parade around like a woman? And, how's he gonna wrestle with fake boobs? They're bound to pop off and fall out. He dove under the bottom rope, rolled into the ring, and jumped up. So far, so good.

He musta been telling the truth when he said Golden Boy Tad was his good friend, because whatever Golden Boy was doing to stay hairless, Uncle Jay was doing, too. He didn't have a single hair on his body either. 'Must be a wrestler's advantage,' I thought.

He appeared pretty out of shape, too. 'When I get home I'll cut out another Charles Atlas coupon, it's only a dime. I can work with him.' I can work with him on this female character, too. It really doesn't work for me. He doesn't have anything even remotely feminine about him.

Whoever did those boobs for him did a good job though. Despite their size, they're not falling out. And, they certainly do jiggle like the real thing. Kudos to the make-up person. Good job. Good job, indeed.

"For a heavy set woman, she's quite agile," said the guy behind me.

"Fooled ya, didn't he. He's my uncle."

"So you said."

"Yeah."

I was applauding Uncle Jay's defensive wrestling moves, which amounted to nothing more than running away from Fabulous Beulah, not that I could really blame him, when the guy behind me, Mr. Head Smacker, stepped over and sat in Uncle Jay's seat.

"Do you have an extra cigarette?"

"You touch me and my uncle'll beat the living crap out of you!"

"Take it easy. I just want a smoke."

"Yeah?"

"Yeah."

"The gold rose ain't for sale."

"Don't want it."

"No?" Leery, but not threatened, cautious, but not rude, I gave him a cigarette.

"You might want to join me."

"Whattya mean by that?"

"You just may want to have one yourself."

I took one for myself. I lit mine and handed the guy my matches. He lit his. I watched as the match grew livelier. He watched the match flicker and die.

"You might want to take a closer look, son."

I stood up amongst three hundred of my closest friends and watched. I stepped up onto my seat for a better look. I didn't have to, but I did. I didn't have to go deaf, dumb, and numb, either. No, I didn't have to, but I did.

My chin didn't have to quiver, my mouth didn't have to waver, my eyes didn't have to narrow, nor did my fixed broad smile fool them all.

"You okay, son?"

"Yeah."

I didn't want to see the obvious. I really didn't want to. Damned if I do, damned if I don't.

"Are you sure you're okay, son?"

"Yeah. Can I ask you a favor?"

"Sure."

"Stop calling me son."

"If that's the way you want it."

"No, that's just the way it is."

The match ended in a blur.

Who won? Who lost? I didn't care.

The cool night air washed over me as we sped home in awkward silence. Even though I had a hundred questions, I couldn't think of anything to say.

"You mean to tell me you never knew?" Uncle Jay/Aunt Judy asked.

"Never."

"Never suspected?"

"Never."

"Nobody ever said a word?"

"Nobody."

"Are you kidding?"

"No."

"Really?"

"Uh-huh."

"Not even the least bit suspicious?"

"Suspicious? You're never around long enough for me to be curious!"

"How about I never went swimming in the lake?" "So?"

"Didn't it seem a little odd?"

"You said you didn't like swimming in the weeds and the muck."

"I don't."

"Well, it's not like you're telling me anything, other than you don't like swimming in the weeds and the muck or maybe you forgot your bathing suit." I reasoned.

"Have you ever seen me write my name in the snow?"

"What has...? Have you ever seen me do that?"

"No, but you can."

"Yeh, so? What would that have proven?"

"That I was what you wanted me to be! Why're you being so difficult?"

"Me?"

"Look, I wasn't hiding anything from anybody. If you didn't know, I'm sorry. Not everything is as it appears, ya know. And very few people are what they appear to be, either."

"But, you make a better guy than most guys."

"No, I just come off better as a male than a female."

"You said I should always be true to myself. Right?"

"Yeah."

"How can you be true to yourself when your life is a lie?"

"I don't think of my life as a lie."

"What would you call it then?"

"I never felt comfortable as a female, I thought my life was a joke. Over time I guess I just got tired of being the punch line."
"What do they call people like you?"

"Uncle Jay."

"But, you're not, not really."

"Then, Aunt Judy."

"This is gonna take awhile."

"Take your time, I'm not going anywhere."

But, she/he was. This was just another innocent, yet truthful, lie. Once I'm dropped off it could be five days, five months, or five years before we see each other again. It all depended on the crime and length of sentence. There was one stretch of time when we didn't see or speak for three years. She told me he had been in the Army. I saw dog tags. But now as I think about it, I was never actually allowed to hold them, to look at them up close. I saw the chain around Uncle Jay's neck, and heard them occasionally clink. It just never crossed my mind they were clinking between a pair of Aunt Judy's boobs.

"Can I ask you something?"

"Of course."

"Um, how do you hide them?" She reached in his bag, tossing me a piece of heavy clothing. I held it up. "What is it?"

"A girdle."

"Don't most ladies wear a girdle?"

"Yeah, just not as high as I do."

"Oh. What are you gonna do now?"

"About what?"

"I dunno. Everything."

"I never found anything I was good at, work wise."

"How 'bout a make-up person?"

"I never touch the stuff," he said, with her best Presley sneerful grin.

"No, but you draw a pretty good moustache," I chuckled.

"Well, thanks, I think."

"A little crooked maybe," both of us laughed.

"I don't know about life, I just hope we can still be friends."

"Yeh, just the three of us. Me, Aunt Jay and Uncle Judy."

"Oh, you're on a roll, aren't ya? I am what I am, smart ass!"

"So's Popeye!" Eventually, the laughing and silliness were replaced by a long, easy, silence. After a few minutes we were talking about Patches and her puppies. About the one male runt who died and the five females who survived when suddenly the obvious hit me. "What about Ronnie?" I asked.

"What about Ronnie?"

"Who's gonna tell her?"

"You still don't quite get it, do ya?"

Chapter 10

Ms. Colmes Studio of Tap & Jazz

Located above the Colonial Theatre in downtown Brockton, Massachusetts, the Mildred Colmes Studio of Tap and Modern Jazz has been a cornerstone in the world of dance for years.

This was the place to be every Saturday morning for Geraldine, Lulu, Cha-Cha, Mimi, my mother, and two sisters.

My younger sister did not take dance lessons. She didn't want to. She found peculiar enjoyment in sitting on the floor in a far corner of the studio, a tap shoe laced to each hand. She would entertain herself for hours doing what can only be described as "hand puppet tap dancing." Parents and dancers smiled as they passed by, commenting on how cute she was. The only time she looked up was when my mother popped another sugar-coated treat in her mouth. It was like she was in a trance. A sugar induced, hand puppet, tap dancing trance.

By never saying a word, my older sister, Patty, made it quite clear she had made it her life's work never to speak to me. When this thought dawned on me I was amused by the stupidity and tried, with humor, to explain such. She slapped me, called me a doofus, and swore I had to be retarded! Though as close to a conversation as I could recall having with her, it was not very

nice. As much as I wanted to be friends, I thought it best to locate her good-natured side another time.

"Why can't you be like your sisters!" my mother would say, more demanding than asking.

Every time she said it the only thought that came to me was, 'Have you taken a look? Have you taken a really good look?'

"And wipe that goddamn smirk off your face! Nobody said anything funny!"

I was also amused at the idea a dance studio would even think, let alone be allowed, to operate above a movie house. It's not like they were teaching ballroom dancing, this was tap, tap dancing!

When it came to individual or even small tap classes, credit had to be given to quality workmanship back in the day. To be fair, in a building this old, the sound-proofing was near perfect. The only time any sounds were heard, was when a group tap happened to be underway. Then it sounded like you were sitting in the midst of a torrential, rain driven, windswept, yet rhythmic, well-choreographed, downpour.

Miss Colmes, owner, aged dance extraordinaire, along with her faithful constantly yipping Pomeranian companion, Fifi, tucked under her arm, held court nights and every Saturday for aspiring Astaire/Rodgers/Rooney/Garland hopefuls.

I did wonder which came first, Geraldine's Lulu or Miss Colmes' Fifi? My money was on Fifi. My spring and summer Saturdays were spent on the Teeny Town baseball field, missing grounders, dropping fly balls, and striking out. When I played at top form I was, at best, mediocre.

But, it was better to be raising hell on a baseball field than stuck in a musty, sweaty, dance studio with mothers, and sisters, and girlfriends of the sisters, and sisters of the girlfriends, and friends of the sisters of the girlfriends, and on, and on, and on.

I had to go one rainy Saturday.

"Do I have to?" was my daring plea.

"Did I ask you?" replied my mother.

"Would you?" I muttered, hopefully.

"Get in the car!" she said, hopes dashed.

As we rode along, I remembered Reggie telling me how, on most Saturdays, because Erwin had to work and Geraldine did not trust Reggie to stay home alone, Geraldine made Reggie go with them to dance class. Once there, she'd send him to the movies where he wouldn't be under foot and get into any trouble.

Reggie had told me about being chased out of the Colonial Theatre by the ushers for swearing at the cartoons, tossing Dots® and Black Crows® at the movie screen, letting kids in the theatre through the fire exits and peeing off the balcony. When asked why he pee'd off the balcony, he claimed he smelled smoke coming from below. I did have my doubts. However, he did shoot the nose-picker with an arrow, and, one night, while Geraldine was home alone, I did witness him prop a large, dead raccoon against the front door of his house and ring the door bell. I thought Geraldine was going to have a heart attack. So, I could not entirely rule out his peeing off the balcony.

Oh, and being chased out of Kresge's Five and Dime for stealing a pack of Black Jack chewing gum.

'So, maybe, for one rainy Saturday, this won't be so bad,' I thought.

I slunk down in a wooden folding chair surrounded by powder and puff, a still fog of hair spray stuff, leopard leotards, mirrored walls, and the incessant sound of, tap-a-tap-a-tap-a-tap-a-tap-a-tap-a-tap, multiplied sixty times by a current class of thirty, multi-aged, multi-proportioned, multi-rhythmless tappers.

I wanted out. 'Too late now.' I wanted Reggie. 'He's not here yet.' I wanted to walk around. 'No, the only place to explore is the backroom and that's the girl's dressing area.' I wanted to look around. 'No, no looking. This room is the girl's dressing area.' I wanted to hide in the boy's bathroom. 'No, there is no boy's bathroom. There is a room with a toilet in it. But, that's also the girl's dressing area.' I wanted to run out. 'No. My mother is standing in the doorway talking to Geraldine.' Well, Reggie can't be too far behind. 'Save me, pal, buddy, chum, Willie-Lump-Lump.'

The class of thirty tapping tornadoes mercifully ended. As they filed into the back dressing area it struck me they couldn't even walk single file in step. They all tap-a-tap-a-tap-a-tapped out to the backroom, out of sync of one another. How could this possibly be?

With Fifi under arm, Miss Colmes made her way to the dance floor, clapping her hands for attention. As she clapped, Fifi yipped, yapped, and flopped about. A red bow, holding a tuft of Fifi's hair up like a mini-volcano eruption, fell off, and Fifi's face disappeared. Fifi looked like a mass of long, fluffy, armpit hair.

Miss Colmes wore her age in deep, heavy facial lines, and even deeper, heavier, blue eye shadow. Her clothes weren't normal. Everything she wore sparkled like she dressed in costume. She was still able to hold her own on the dance floor but, because of her age, only danced at the yearly recital.

The tap dance instructors were all former dance students. They were paid to ready any and all fleet-footed, flat-footed wannabes, with money in hand to pay for the lessons, for the annual spring recital held at the Brockton High School auditorium. Rumor was every one of the instructors had a wee bit of a drinking problem. From what I had just witnessed, the reasons were obvious.

Cha-Cha, Mimi, and my sister, Patty, stood huddled in a corner, glancing in my direction, pointing, whispering and giggling. 'Reggie stayed home and I'm stuck here all alone, all day, right? Right? That's not funny!'

128

The girl's boyfriends strolled in and, for a moment, every female hormone in the place started tapping, until the three girls moved in to claim their property. The six of them were all kissy-face. Geraldine looked at them and grinned. She nudged my mother who looked and gave a painted grin, until Geraldine looked away, then she looked back at my sister with her scornful scowl.

My mother did not like Patty's boyfriend. She did like his money though. His family was loaded. Curious enough, the money would be the cause of their break-up in a roundabout way. It was a case of multi-insecurity and multi-jealousy, with a reality chaser.

Patty loved being showered with all the baubles and trinkets; she would show my mother each and every one. It didn't take long for my mother to suggest the money was "being wasted on such nonsense," and would be put to better use if Patty got the cash, then my mother would "invest" it.

The guy was loaded with money, not stupidity.

Patty was loaded, too, unfortunately, not with money.

While driving home one day, she made the dopey mistake of showing off his parent's home. They didn't go in, they just drove past. It wasn't a huge estate, but a very nice home. Well-manicured, well-maintained, a beautiful piece of property. A mini-estate. Then again to my mother, any house, as long as it was not maroon with a blue roof and sagging in the middle, was a mini-estate. Not that we talked about it, I just knew. And, somehow, I knew she knew I knew, too.

Mini-estate. Sad, saggy, year-round summer house. Haves, have-nots.

I knew my mother was overwhelmed. In her mind, his folks were the same as those who bought the cottages. People who owned winter homes within the city limits, yet invaded her year round slice of, sliver of, suburban paradise every Memorial Day. Tormenting her, just by living, until Labor Day. And live they did!

129

There were parties and cook-outs, Fourth of July festivities, and more than a few beer blasts. Raucous laughter. Old friends. New friends. Midnight swims. Relatives. Reunions. New vacationing families. Old vacationing families. Good-spirited, memory lasting, Rockwell summers by the lake. My dead-end street came alive!

And, okay, yes, at times, an occasional bout of drunken revelry. Those are the moments my mother would see. "Goddamn drunk pissing on his cottage!" And she wondered why we were never invited to any of the summer bashes. Ever.

In her mind, my mother saw the whole picture. Soon she would have to attend, unattended, a "meet the parents" dinner party at the mini-estate, not that one had even been mentioned. Then, of course, there would "have to be" a reciprocal gala at the sad, saggy, maroon, year round summer house with the blue roof. And the snowball kept rolling.

The reality chaser? There on display for all their monetary status, one on the front lawn of the mini-estate and two in the backyard by the pool, three, cast iron, reindeer! My mother was laid up for weeks with a severe case of self-put-upon, self-diagnosed, "reindeer recall."
My sister's cash cow was trampled by a trio of, a mini-herd of, Rudolphs!

Now, with the boyfriends arrival, I have someone to talk to, or so I thought. The girls pointed to the backroom and the boyfriends headed to the rear dressing area. I thought to tell them, 'There's no boy's room back there,' but, oh well, they'll see.

"All modern jazzers to the floor please," Miss Colmes requested.

Patty, Mimi, and Cha-Cha, made their way to the dance floor. Geraldine and my mother smiled at one another as their daughters took their positions.

Suddenly, with no prompting, for no reason other than she could, Cha-Cha did a kick and a spin, ending up in a full floor split. A squeal and a round of applause came from Geraldine. My mother gave a half-hearted smile and less than enthusiastic clap. She glared at Patty and scowled. Patty glanced away. She wasn't as big a flaunt as Cha-Cha, more so than Mimi, for sure, but, neither of them, or any of the other dancers for that matter, could hold a candle to Cha-Cha. Not one of them could fill Cha-Cha's leotard and Patty was not going to make a fool of herself just to please my mother.

I tilted, slowly, to one side to get a better look at Cha-Cha limbering up while still in a full split. She held out her arms and bending slowly, touched her forehead to her knee. She sat back erect. Then, arms still extended, she bent forward at the waist and shook her shoulders, and everything else. Patty and Mimi stood off to the side. They'd seen this sideshow a thousand times before.

Knowing she was the center of attention, Cha-Cha then half turned sharply left, then sharply right, then left again. Then, with no effort, she lifted slightly off the floor and did a complete about face. She bounced her bum off the floor five or six times. Everything about her jiggled. I had this funny feeling I shouldn't be watching while, at the same time, I felt I had to.

Just as I broke the spell and looked away, my mother caught my eye and shot me her, *'What the hell you looking at?'* face. This is going to be a no-win day. 'Where in hell is Reggie?'

"All modern jazzers to the floor," Miss Colmes announced.

Three girls sitting near to me, about my age, maybe a little older, got up and went to the dance floor. From the backroom came the boyfriends. I scooted down to make room for the guys to sit with me but they walked right by and lined up with the now, six girls.

'This is getting a little weird,' I thought.

"That's *all modern jazzers!*" Miss Colmes and Fifi both barked.

131

I looked over my shoulder and who finally came bounding out of the backroom but, Willie-Lump-Lu--, I mean Reggie. 'Finally, I can get the hell out of here,' I thought.

I started to get up. Reggie spotted me and looked away, pretending he didn't see me, as he hustled to the dance floor. I wanted to say, "Hey, where you going? And, why are you wearing your old Cub Scout summer shorts?" But, I have never been able to laugh hilariously and speak at the same time. He was actually hustling to the dance floor! He never hustled in his life! This has to be a joke! How can he dance when he can't even run? Is this why he quit playing baseball? I knew he felt bad for getting picked off the bases, constantly. And, when he did play, he'd play catcher, not because he could catch a pitched ball, but he sure could stop them. Never saw one get by him. Never saw him actually catch one, but, I never saw one get by him either. Reggie wasn't huge; he was, um, big boned, with a lot of layers on them bones.

Miss Colmes looked to the dance floor then turned to the backroom. "Six girls, four boys? That's all modern jazzers, *now!*" Fifi cringed.

And the lucky winner of Miss Colmes' wrath is, '*Oh my dear sweet Jes..I'll be a son-of-a-bit...it's the nose-picker!*' What the fu--? At the start of the season he was our pitcher, our best pitcher, then he quit. He was on the mound, in the middle of a game, in the middle of a pitch, when he just stopped in mid-motion and yelled out, "It's too hot!" Then he stuck his glove under his arm, stuck his thumb out for a ride, and stuck a finger up his nose. That was the last I saw of him, until now.

"We have six girls, five boys," Miss Colmes said to no one, except Fifi I guess.

'Wait til the guys on the team hear about this,' I thought, trying hard not to laugh aloud.

"We're one short."

'They are not going to believe this.'

132

"Any of you girls know where our sixth boy is?"

'They'll both be laughed off the bus. Run out of school.'

"We have a sixth boy right here, Miss Colmes."

I was laughing so hard I couldn't breathe. I needed air. I had to go. I had to get out. I stood to leave. 'Who just spoke?' I turned, stepping right into my mother.

"Wha--? Oh, no!" I exclaimed.

"Oh, no? Oh, no, what?" asked my mother, a twisted smile on her face.

"Oh, no, no, no, no!" Everyone laughed.

To the unknowing, it looked like she set a mother's loving arm on her son's shoulder to support him in his moment of despair. When in fact, she slyly gripped the back of my neck and squeezed, not releasing until she had walked me onto the dance floor.

"Find your partner," Miss Colmes said. "No, not Cha-Cha."

Cha-Cha took hold of my skinny kid shoulders and to everyone's delight, yanked me to her big boobs. She held firm to the back of my head and shook.

'I've never been this close before!' I thought. The gods were truly having their way with me.

I was gasping for air when my wad of Black Jack chewing gum *gushed* from my mouth onto her cleavage. I quickly *slurped* it back into my mouth. She spoke in a high, babyish tone, "There, there, little guy, we'll be gentle with you."

She spun me about, now I faced my sister. Patty stopped laughing. Her glare screamed, *'Don't touch me, don't talk to me,*

don't even know me!' I looked to Mimi for help, she pointed to the three younger girls.

I looked toward the girls and saw only two, the third girl hid behind her friends. As I walked past Reggie, I asked if he had seen any good movies lately. 'Liar.' He just laughed.

Walking past the nose-picker, I walked faster. Reggie came and stood by his partner. The nose-picker came over, gnawing away at his fingernails, and stood near his.

"Theeth min," said the nose-picker.

"Huh?"

"Theeth min, a thed."

"What?"

"She's mine, I said!" He was very annoyed and very loud.

"Well, stop eating your fingers!" He renewed his gnawing to spite me.

"Eu doun liki? Tsuf!"

"What?"

"You don't like it? Tough!" Right then, I knew we would never be friends.

The third girl was still hiding, crouched behind the four of them. Either she was very shy, or, she did not want to be seen with me. Shyness is so debilitating. They all giggled and laughed. Finally, she stepped out from behind them. Of the three girls she was the nicest looking. Older, fourteen, fifteen, with shiny, shoulder length dark hair, dark eyes, a bob of a nose, just a hint of make-up, a shy smile, and nice teeth. Her boobs weren't as big as Cha-Ch--.

"Hi, I'm Roxanne. Can you do a shuffle ball change?"

134

I had no idea what she just said to me. I figured it had to have something to do with dancing.

"No. Can you snag a screaming line drive off the top of your shoelaces, drop, roll, and come up throwing to the plate?" She had no idea what I was talking about. "We're even, partner."

Before the day was over I realized I had learned two new things. I shuffle ball changed until I knew how to shuffle ball change.

And, I knew there was not one kid on my baseball team I could ever share this with.

Everyone was leaving.

My mother and I stood at either side of the exit doors in silence, waiting for Geraldine. She scowled. I couldn't tell if it was her happy scowl or her mad scowl. I was having trouble telling one from the other.

Well, if no one else was happy, Miss Colmes was. She gave me a hug and said I did a great job. Over Fifi's yipping I heard her say something about, "Having another boy in the class."

"I play baseball Saturdays. Today rained."

She smiled at my mother and walked away. My mother gave me her sour look. I couldn't tell if it was her happy sour look or her mad sour look. Lately, I was having trouble with this look, too.

Did she think I was coming back next Saturday? Saturday is for my baseball. I know how to hold a bat, not a girl!

Roxanne smiled at me when she was leaving. As she neared, her lips puckered slightly. For a split second I was caught off guard. Looking her right in the eye as she approached, I held her look, puckering a slow pucker in return. Then, just as she was beside me, I heard her softly whisper, "practice." My pucker melted, I nodded and smiled. 'Well, that was embarrassing,' I thought. 'It's okay.

135

She'll be the one embarrassed next Saturday, shuffle ball changing with no partner.'

The boyfriends had their own cars, so the girls, including my younger sister, still wearing her tap shoe mittens, left with them. Erwin had stopped by earlier taking Reggie and the nose-picker with him.

"Did you have fun today?" Geraldine asked, as we pulled into traffic.

"Was okay." 'Why's she with us? Why's she talkin' to me? Why'm I ridin' with them?'

"Miss Colmes thought it was really good you came today. She told me you and Roxanne did pretty good, too. You need to work on the shuffle ball change. That can be a tricky step. Mimi and Patty did good. They need to be looser. Loosen it up. The boyfriends are doing a nice job. Reggie is working very hard. For just his third week, Davey was right there on every step, every step. I thought he did a very, very good job. Very good job. He's a talented kid, Davey. You can see it in him. If you lose the step, just look at Davey."

"Who's Davey?"

"The kid next door, you fool," my mother said, annoyed.

"Huh? Oh." The nose-picker. Why didn't they just say so?

"What, you never knew his name?" asked my mother, an edginess in her voice.

"Well, yeah, but, I was told it a while ago."

"Don't be stupid. He didn't change his name. What do you call him when you talk to him?"

'nose-picker' "I don't know. I never talk to him."

136

"Weren't you two on the same baseball team this year?" Geraldine piped up.

"Yeah, for a little while."

"What, you never talked to him?" asked my mother in a challenging tone.

"Well, yeah, but..." Why'm I getting the third degree?

"So, what did you call him?"

"I didn't call him anything. He's a pitcher. He talks to pitchers." Now I see where this is going.

"So, what did they call him?"

And here we are. It's like being careful to look first before you cross the railroad tracks. Even though you're careful, so careful you look both ways, twice, when you step on the tracks, a speeding freight train *slams* into you anyway! It's not your fault you didn't see it coming, but, it is your fault you didn't see the tracks being laid.

"Nose-picker."

"*If I ever hear you called him that, I--,*" she exploded.

"Not me, th--"

"*Did you, did you call him that? Did you?*"

"No, the pitchers! The other guys!"

"*Don't ever let me hear you say that! Understood?*"

"Yes." 'nose-picker, nose-picker, nose-picker, nose-picker, nose-picker, nose-picker, nose-picker, nose-picker, nose-picker, nose-picker, nose-picker, nose-picker, nose-picker, nose-picker, nose-picker, nose-picker, nose-picker, nose-picker, nose-picker, nose-

picker, nose-picker, nose-picker, nose-picker, nose-picker, nose-picker, nose-pic--'

"My Cha-Cha is such a terror. Isn't my Cha-Cha a terror, Edna? Damn terror is what she is. And strong, God, that girl is strong. Took the three boys to throw her in the lake last night. All three of them. Took all they could to get her on the ground. Just to get her on the ground. The boyfriend tried holding her down. She got him off. Grabbed him right there. She got him off. Right there. You know, there? He let go pretty quick. Pretty quick, I tell you. He won't be so grabby again too soon. Not again. Not too soon again, no. Damn near tore the bottoms right off her. He did! Damn near. Only got a rip, just a rip, little rip up the side. Just the side, up the seam. How's your headache, Edna? Do you think we can get him something else to wear next week, Edna? All day long all I hear is corduroy rubbing. Rubbing, rubbing. All day, rubbing. I thought he was gonna catch on fire," Geraldine said, and they laughed hysterically.

"I play baseball on Saturday. Every Saturday til school starts." My mother eye-balled me in the rearview and squinted. I looked away, staring out the window.

"You said there were two weeks left. That's what you said. Remember? I remember. Wasn't it, Edna? Two weeks? Now what is it? Four games? Five? What's it now? Four, five weeks? A month? Is that right? Miss Colmes can't wait a month, Edna. You should've told her he does not want to. He's not going to do it. Do you play good? Reggie never played good, that's why he's doing the dancing. I told him he would be better to do the dancing, he put on the weight doing the baseball, sitting on the bench every game. Reggie said he played when you played. Reggie never played. When do you play?" she inhaled.

"Ev-er-y Sat-ur-day," I said slow, clear, mechanical.

"*Why do you have to be so?*" my mother said, slamming the brakes.

"She asked when I played," I pleaded.

"Sh, sh, Edna. It's alright. It's alright." My mother sped up. "Too bad it's *ev-er-y Sat-ur-day* though." Geraldine's mocking, said in such a drawled and drooly way, made the words even smell bad.

"That's it! No more baseball! Season's over!" I knew the tone. It's over. I didn't so much as make a peep the rest of the way home. Geraldine coddled my mother by asking about her mythical lifelong headache.

'You wanna talk headache, crazy lady? I've got the headache! Why don't you talk to me? You gave it to me! Don't even talk to me!' I wanted to scream.

We drove past my house, down the short dirt road, pulling into Geraldine's gully pocked driveway. She didn't get out. Didn't even try. They just sat, motor running, making small talk. They weren't talking to me. My house is right over there. I'm home. I opened the door.

"Where the hell you think you're going? Shut the door," my mother said. "Shut the door!" Geraldine looked at me and scowled. Leering in the rearview, my mother saw me look at Geraldine. *"I said shut the goddamn door!"* I pulled the door shut and slid down. "Sit up. I said, sit up! Keep it up, you'll lose more than baseball! Hear me? Do you hear me? I still have a bone to pick with you."

"Why don't you take mum home and make her a nice hot cocoa?" 'Why don't you go fry your arse in buttermilk!' I thought, tickled at another of my li'l black dad's phrases.

"He doesn't care! As long as he gets to do what he wants to do, that's all he cares about. Right? *Right?*"

No one had arrived at either house, yet. Just us, and we sat. I wondered where everybody was? Where they went? What they were doing? Why was I here? Not so much the girls, Erwin and Reggie mainly. I never saw them do any father and son stuff. Erwin still worked plenty, still worked the two jobs, custodian and pizza maker supporting their brood. He's such an easy-going guy I

figured he'd be good to go fishing with, take a ride with, or just talk to.

Something. Anything. When dark clouds gathered, I dreamt of a life anywhere else.

"So you'll get to the bottom of the other?" asked Geraldine with a scowl.

My mother nodded.

'What? Bottom of what other?'

Geraldine pushed the door open and, in a most un-ladylike manner, she wriggled, squirmed, twisted and turned, trying to escape the adhesive grip the plastic seat cover had on the back of her legs. Eventually, the plastic lost the battle and *ripped* free from her stubby calves, her sweaty thighs. They laughed. I didn't. Geraldine plodded to her front door, waved and slammed the jalousie door shut.

My mother put the car in reverse, we slowly backed up. "What the...?" She braked, eyeing where Geraldine had sat. "What is that?"

"What?" I leaned forward, looking to the front seat, *bam,* her elbow bashed my forehead.

"What the hell are you doing?" she barked.

"You said to look," I said, clutching at a soon to be goose egg.

"I did not! I said, 'What is that?' Not, 'Look at that!'" She brushed the fictitious bit of, piece of, pile of, glob of *nothing* off the seat. She turned to look out the rear window. I ducked. "What'sa matter? Why're you cringing? You want to cringe; I'll give you something to cringe for. And you roll your goddamn eyes one more time and I'll roll your ass right out of this car! I don't give a shit who's watching! Hear me? *Do you hear me?"*

I dreamt of living with Jackie and JFK. She parked. I jumped out.

"Patches? Patches? Here girl. Patches, c'mon girl."

"Get in the house."

"Patches was loose when we left."

"Get in the house. Get up to your room." I looked at her. "Did I say get in the house? Get in the house!"

"What'd I do?" I said, going to the living room. "I didn't do anything."

"Is that your room? I said your room!" she yelled from the kitchen.

"Why?" I pleaded, nursing my forehead. She picked up a kitchen chair, slammed it down, then raced into the living room.

"You don't ask! You do! Now, *Go!*" I avoided walking too near and started up the stairs to my hall.

"Keep it up; go ahead, you'll lose more than baseball."

Out of gnashed teeth - "I" - youthful conviction - "did" - confusion - "not" - between a drop of sweat - "do" - the roll of a tear - "any"- and years of frustrated innocence - "thing!" I sighed a long, weary sigh. And she was on me.

I was four or five steps up when she rushed over, clutching and pulling the back cuff of my corduroys, dropping me full-length flat, forehead first. She yanked me back, down the hard, rubber tread covered, wooden stairs. 'That hurt and it's gonna leave a mark. Think! *Think!*' Two survival modes came to mind: Land on your side and curl up. I hit the floor landing on my side and curled up. Her meaty knee drove down, crunching the arm protecting my ribs. She forced me into the base of the first step by crashing her knee into my back. She rolled me over, pinning my arms across my chest with her knee, rendering me helpless with her solid body

141

weight. A ball of flesh slammed my temple at the hairline. Five pudgy fingers raked my face left to right, the other five, right to left. She stopped and stared down on me. She didn't move. I didn't move. I never moved. I stared back, right back into her eyes. 'Where's the glint, where's the flicker, where's the fucking light?' I screamed, silently. 'There. There it is.' She got up. 'That went pretty quick. Thank God for little favors.'

She went to the kitchen.

I got up, not knowing what, when, where, or why. This was the riddle. What, did I do? When, did I do it? Where, is she going to explode next? And, 'Why?' Just once, give me one good reason why.

"Let me see your forehead," she said. "Come here. You're okay," she assured me. "Get over here." I tilted forward, rocked back. "Now! It's okay." She ran cold water on a dishtowel, went to tilt my head back, I ducked. "I said it's okay," she draped my forehead and eyes with the towel. "I told you not to run up the stairs," she said, pressing at the towel. "When you're cleaned up I want you to go outside and find Patches."

"Okay."

"And I think you should take the dance classes."

"But..." I squirmed. She held the towel in place.

"And I want you to say you're sorry to Cha-Cha for licking her chest."

I tried wriggling free. I wanted to explain. She pressed the towel on my face from chin to forehead with one hand, holding firm the back of my head with the other. I went still. She removed the towel.

"I love you. Now go outside."

Another normal day in Eden.

142

Chapter 11

The Recital

The recital was in six weeks.

With the girls, the boyfriends, the nose-picker, Reggie and me, all doing the same routine, the exact same steps, along with rehearsing practically in my backyard at Reggie's Great Gray Monster a coupla times a week, this would be a cinch.

Wrong, wrong, wrong! I was oh, so wrong!

First off, Reggie's partner, the nose-picker's partner, and Roxanne, because of the distance, and because they were too young to drive, never attended the Great Gray Monster rehearsals. And second, the only dance the girls, including my sister and the boyfriends had in mind when we would get together to rehearse, was the horizontal bop.

This left Reggie, the nose-picker, and me, partnerless. We tried, but, oh, I don't know, something about shuffle ball changing with Reggie wasn't right. And, as hard as I tried to see the nose-picker as a Davey, he was always going to be the nose-picker to me.

It seemed a waste of time without Roxanne.

So, when they wanted us to disappear, we'd blackmail the boyfriends for cigarettes and smoke out behind Reggie's house, huddled behind the huge propane tank we called the H-Bomb.

On Saturdays I'd stick to Roxanne like glue and rehearse and practice, again and again. Not because I was enjoying dance over baseball, but I was becoming a bit "smitten" with Roxanne. This is the word my Grandma Millie would use. 'Look at the little bunghole will ya, all smitten.'

I asked Roxanne why she acted so shy the first Saturday. She said she was only pretending to be shy, but she was a little embarrassed everybody knew she was the one without a partner. She did feel bad the way I was tricked and dragged into the group though. She knew I didn't want to be there. I told her I was sorry and hoped she didn't take it personally. She understood. She understood everything.

Roxanne was sweet and kind and sensitive, looked really cute in a leotard, and she didn't smell like Avon, Old Spice, or vinaigrette. 'Look at the bunghole will ya, all smitten.'

Then she said the real reason she didn't have a partner was Reggie and Davey met her jealous boyfriend and he would be coming to the recital, but right after the show she was going to dump him. She suspected he knew of her plans and he'd do something to embarrass her the night of the show. I told her as long as she was with me she need not worry about a thing. If anyone was to worry, he should be the one looking over his shoulder. Then I saw him. He was huge. I told her she was on her own.

The show was billed as a night of "song and dance."

Come to find out, the "singers" were old cronies, as my mother and Geraldine referred to them, from back in Miss Colmes' Off-Broadway dance hall days. I wondered whether the singers felt as bad for the dancers who couldn't, as I felt for the singers who no longer could?

The show was set so there was a couple of dance numbers, a singer, couple of dance numbers, singer, etc. Then a rousing finale would bring everyone on stage for a final bow. My number was set towards the end of the program.

There was a definite energy, magic in the air, with all the people, the costumes, the make-up, the hustle 'n bustle, the energy, the camaraderie.

'Ladies 'n Gents, Boys 'n Girls, Sapiens 'n Sexuals, it's Showtime.'

The wait was excruciating.

During intermission, I peeked through the curtains slit and saw all the people. Selling tickets to, talking about, just using the word "Audience" for the past six weeks, did little to really prepare me for them all to actually show up.

Miss Colmes, the consummate pro, worked the crowd, Fifi tucked under her arm. She looked quite nice, all decked out in sparkly blue sequins with her newly coifed hair-do. Miss Colmes looked quite spiffy also.

Roxanne's boyfriend sat in the front row, lying in wait for me to do something stupid with Roxanne, so he could give me a good thumping.

My mother, younger sister, Liz, and Grandma Millie, sat a couple of rows back. Liz and my Grandma Millie were having a good laugh about something or other. They were obviously having a good time. My mother sat there, all grumpy. So, she was having a good time too.

Erwin had just arrived, coming right from his job, still in his work clothes. He stood in the back of the auditorium, smiling, nodding.

Geraldine was nowhere to be seen. She was a stage mom through and through, always lurking somewhere behind the lights.

Though the balcony was closed, I caught the shadowy glimpse of someone leaning over the balconies brass rail, inching along, looking down on the crowd. It was Reggie. 'He wouldn't dare! But, then again…' I watched as he slowly walked out the exit door.

The thought of the possible disaster Reggie was capable of, the long minutes I had to anticipate the calamity before he finally left the balcony, the excitement of the evening, the nerves; everything was having an effect on me. 'I gotta pee.'

There were five numbers to go before my number was up.

On my way to the boy's room, as I slipped in and out of the backstage darkness, I saw waiting in the wings, a tall, slender, strikingly attractive, older woman, who looked like she could be on any stage, any professional stage, certainly not this high school auditorium. I knew she had to be a singer. I knew she was next on deck. I knew I had to pee, but, I also knew, at least I felt, and I really don't know why, I had to hear her sing a little bit of her song.

The tappers, tap-a-tap-a-tap-a-tapped, in unison I might add, off the stage. Of course, one of the youngest of the bunch, cute as a button, complete with springy Shirley Temple finger curls, broke away from the bunch, tap ran her way to the lip of the stage, peered out over the footlights and yelled, "How was that, mommy?"

The audience loved her improv. As cute as the moment was, I immediately understood why you should never share the stage with cute little kids. Or animals. Either one will steal the show by just being natural.

The lights dimmed. When they came back up, the lady was standing in the soft blue haze of baby spotlights. The band started off slowly, the tune known by all immediately. If this were "Name That Tune" everyone would've won. She came in on the song softly and everybody knew, I knew, this was going to be special.

"Rock-a-bye your baby, with a Dixie melody,"

Some singer, Eddie Cantor I think his name was, very popular back in my li'l black dad's day, recorded it. Over the years it had become a classic.

"And when you croon, croon a tune, right from the heart of Dixie."

I don't know why, or what it was, maybe a bit of everything, her voice, her style, her presence, grace, calm, and confidence, her total command of this, her moment in the spotlight, I don't know, but the stage was hers, she made it so.

"Just hang my cradle, mammy mine, right on that Mason Dixon line,
And swing it from Virginia, to Tennessee with all the love that's in ya."

She was more than a singer. She was an artist with an understanding of theatre dramatics and stage dynamics. For the first time in my life I was lost in more than hitting a ninth inning, game winning, home run. Not that I ever did.

"Weep no more my baby, when you sing that song for me.
And Old Black Joe, just as though, you had me on your knee."

The auditorium was silent. Alone in the wings, I had the best seat in the house. Her voice, her delivery, was different, special, original. I was hearing, seeing, a real singer. A bonafide star. I got all goose-bumps. 'I really gotta pee!'

"A million baby-kisses I'll deliver,
The minute that I hear you sing that Swanee River."

I knew the song well enough to know this was not the time to go, it had a helluva finish if done properly, but, when ya gotta go, ya gotta go. I made my way deeper in the dimly lit backstage area.

'That's odd,' I thought. The further I made my way from her, the richer, more distinct, I heard her wonderful voice. How? I was walking away from her, not heading toward her.

147

'What's this?'

"Rock-a-bye your rock-a-bye baby with a Dixie melody..."

Set off in a corner of the deepest, darkest backstage area, a circle of heavy black curtains hung. A wire, a cord, snaked under, causing a curtain to rise and part, just enough so light trickled out. The curtains encircled and intentionally hid whatever was going on behind them. This was so out of place. Obviously, it was private, secret. 'I'll reward my curiosity now, pee in a minute.'

"Oh, rock-a-bye your baby, with a Dixie melody..."

Was Cha-Cha doing something with her boyfriend? Or Mimi, the quiet one, busting loose? Or was it my sister? Gross! I moved with feline stealth, with care, caution, with anxious apprehension. My bladder would surely burst.

"When you croon, croon a tune, right from the heart of Dixie..."

Standing inches from where the ray of light teased me to peek in, I saw a tall, thin figure, dressed in white. 'What the hell?' I moved closer. Whoever it was, they were transfixed. Staring. Ogling. 'Oh, my God, it's Erwin!' He was standing there, still in his work clothes, still in his pepperoni and pizza sauce stained whites.

"Just hang my cradle, mammy mine, right on that Mason Dixon line,
And swing it from Virginia, to Tennessee with all the love that's in ya."

Standing at a microphone with eyes shut, arms extended, wearing a black muumuu dress, was Geraldine, belting out every note, every word, with every ounce of heartfelt passion the woman could possibly pull from her soul.

"Aw-w, weep no more my baby, aw-w when you sing that song for me..."

Geraldine supplied the voice the woman on stage did not have. The woman on stage supplied the look the audience would expect that voice to have. I stared in disbelief. I was in awe. Stunned. Riveted. I even forgot I had to pee.

"And Old Black Joe, just as though, you ha-aaad me on your knee..."

Her body shook, her muumuu rippled, as she gave her private audience of two a performance worthy of encore and standing ovation. She bent back, the lyrics flowed out freely. I felt every ounce of emotion pour from her.

"A million baby kisses I'll deliver...
The minute that I hear you sing that Swanee River..."

Her gray hair slid smoothly across the back of her black muumuu. Her jowls shook with total abandon as she called upon every pore, every facet of her being, to make that aging lady on stage a star for three minutes.

"Oh-h, rock-a-bye, your rock-a-bye baby, with a Di-x-ie Mel-o-deeeeee."

Geraldine held the last note, caring, caressing, protecting, to the extent a mother protects her child, even as she sets it free. Over, the air was still. Silent.

The audience broke like a slow rolling wave. Gaining, growing, strengthening. Roaring to a raucous ear-splitting crescendo of unbridled love through applause.

Erwin pulled a hanky from his pizza cook pants and wiped his face and eyes.

Geraldine stood in time suspended, bathed in the spotlight of the 200 watt light bulb, basking in the warmth and adulation of her unseen audience. She stepped back from the microphone as Erwin went to her. He bent down to give the woman of his life an all-inclusive kiss; she returned his love ten-fold. Their embrace lasted

as long as the audience expressed their gratitude.

I may have been just a snot-nosed kid, but I damn near cried. I wanted to rush in and hug, too. I wanted to take back every bad thought I ever had of the crazy lady. I wanted to tell the audience the truth. I wanted to, but, as my li'l black dad would say, 'I gotta pee like a racehorse!'

Four numbers to go. I grabbed and squeezed as only a kid who has to go real bad is allowed to grab and squeeze. Silently, I shuffle ball changed from the curtains, the lovers, the backstage.

When I finally made it to the hallway, I ran like hell for the boy's room.

Having never been in this school before I had no idea what hall led where. I was a mouse in a maze. I was waddling like a duck. I held my breath. Little noises escaped me. Tiny grunts and high squeals. 'To hell with it. If I'm reduced to a barnyard animal, I'll pee in a water bubbler!'

My search had taken me so far away from the stage area; I could no longer hear the music. I turned yet another corner when, finally, about fifty yards ahead, a "BOYS" sign. I was so relieved I feared I would be too relieved.

My one quart bladder was three quarts full!

Desperate, frantic, contorted in agony, I scuffled to the door, grasped the handle with my sweaty hand and yanked. And yanked!?! And pulled?!? And yanked!!!

My sweaty, drippy grip ripped free from the locked door's handle, lashed back, walloping my face dead center, square on my nose. Crumbled, defeated, I lay in a semi-conscious nirvana stupor for an eternal minute. I rolled to my knees groping at airy images of faceless souls extending helping hands, tossing life preservers to a drowning boy. I dragged my head across the bloodied floor's cool tile for a reunion with its body.

In total disillusion I sat there, reeling in a puddle of my own me.

I felt like a swan in a swamp.

For a brief moment, I was hysterical. 'What'd I do to deserve this? My life just flashed before my eyes and it was just a snapshot! I have not been alive long enough to piss anyone off this much.' And then it passed. The only words which came to mind were words I heard my li'l black dad utter to my mother on many of her stressed-out occasions, "Geesus, get a grip-poli!"

Oh, sure, his words seem simple, even seem obvious now, but it took a tube of Grandma Millie's denture adhesive for me to realize just how obvious, just how simple, those words were. I stood on shaky, fragile legs, in an attempt to take stock of any positives I had going in my favor. Any positives. Any positives at all!

The wide reflective border around the school lockers mirrored bloody smears up the bridge of my nose, between my eyes, smudged across my forehead, up and into my hairline. 'Not bad, not bad at all. It'll wash off in the bubbler.'

Next, if only my black dress pants didn't have a sheen, an all over shiny wet look. If only they didn't cling like a second skin. Get past that, my pants were fine.

I pulled at the white polo shirt which, along with the black pants, completed my dance attire. Looking down on it, inspecting, expecting major damage, I was flush with luck not seeing as much as a hint of a blood...drop! I watched it spread center of my shirt, like a bulls-eye, to the size of a quarter. I thought the feeling welling up inside of me was what a nervous breakdown feels like at this tender age, or, this was going to be a well-deserved release of a good cry, but I erred. I sneezed. I looked like a walking inkblot test card.

Obviously the gods aren't done with me yet,' I thought.

walked from my man-made lily pond looking like I'd come out

on the short end of three minutes with Fabulous Beulah. My socks squished in my shoes with each step. My nose hurt and would flow free a bloody stream if I didn't keep sniffling and swallowing back.

And, something smelled funny? 'Me!'

I'm disgusted! This is disgusting! And I'm the disgustee!

'Will somebody please help me?' I heard myself scream, softly.

I had to be going over the edge. In my head I was hearing bits of Coach, Erwin, even my Uncle Aunt Judy Jay all speaking the same words to me. 'C'mon, boy, it's the ninth inning, two outs, bases loaded. Your team is down by a run and you're up. This is no time to throw in the towel. This is when real men pull themselves up by their boot-strings, look fate square in the eye, sneer a cock-sure sneer, fart, and huck a louie!' But, the only face I saw was my li'l black dad.

I walked on, trying to retrace my steps out of this devil's maze. I walked faster, pulling at the pullover, pulling it off. I started running.

'Yeah, that's the spirit, boy! That's the ticket!' I heard my li'l black dad say.

I heard music. My music. I turned my shirt inside out. The blood spots went right through, but only on the front. 'I'll wear it backwards, tuck in the collar, and I won't turn around.'

I ran at full speed towards the music. My music. Sure I know I'm late, but I've worked too hard the last six weeks. This is my time, my moment, my music. Better late than never. I still have time to put a smile on Roxanne's face. On Miss Colmes' face. On my mother's face.' Well, two out of three ain't bad.

As I ran, I made a plan. 'I'll follow the music, find the stage, wait until Roxanne shuffle ball changes stage left, take her hand, and just appear on stage in step with her. Then, stage left? My right, her stage left is her right, wait. My left is my stage right! NO! Her

152

stage right is my right? NO! 'Wipe the blood off your face!' RUN-RUB-RUN-RUB-RUN-RUB-RUN 'I'll never make it! NO! YES! NO!' RUN-RUB 'I HAVE TO MAKE IT!' RUB-RUN 'NO!' RUN-RUB-RUN 'YES!'

Better to run a race and find yourself a loser, than quit and find a failure.

'Where 'n hell did that come from?'

Turn-Corner-Slip-Turn-Corner-Slip-Turn-Cor-BA-BAM!

The soles of my shoes slipped out from under me. I slammed into the hard tile, sprawling on the floor. The floor did not give an inch. I came to just enough, just in time to hear music, my music, fade away.

Roxanne's ghost danced in my head. Solo. All alone. All by herself. The monster with a thousand eyes giggled, chuckled, laughed aloud, taunting, pointing at poor Roxanne. She danced naked for all to leer at, under the pitiless glare of the unforgiving spotlight, going it alone like the trooper she was.

Both of my sisters' silent images shot by. Twelve wordless years would! Tonight pretty much rubber-stamps twelve more. 'Maybe, maybe we just have nothing in common. Maybe they're both adopted? Maybe.'

Telling the truth is not an option. If I told one person the truth and it got back to my mother, the truth would not let me see the light of a new day.

When the truth won't work, when no excuse, no explanation will do, when all is desperate and lost and you have nothing left to lose, pray. Pray for a miracle!

Then be patient.

Sometimes they do come.

Chapter 12

Miracle Patches

"I didn't do it on purpose, it was an accident!"

"Wake-up!" Slap. "How many were there?" Slap.

"Where are they?"

"I won't do it again, I promise I'll be good!"

"Kid? You okay?" Slap.

"You said take her to the vegetarian. He killed her!"

"Yeah, okay." Slap. "Hey kid, snap out of it!"

"I didn't mean to do it! Stop the hitting!"

"Who did this? Give me a name?"

"Patches."

"Patches, uh-huh." Slap, slap.

"Yiiiieee, stop! Stop the slapping!"

"You okay? Who did this? How many?"

"Who? How? Who you?"

"Take a deep breath. You're all right, they're gone. I'm Lenny, the night custodian. You okay? You're a mess. How many were they?"

"Uh, how many?"

"Yeah, one? Two? You didn't do this to yourself."

"Three."

"Cowardly bastards!"

"Yeah."

Lenny was a short, thin, wiry individual, with veins for arms, and a half a tube a day Brylcreem® habit. Mid-forties. He wore his green custodial garb and spit-shined black work boots like a man in uniform.

"You're okay now. Alright?"

"Yeah."

"Why are you back here? You part of the show? Dancer?"

"Yeah. No! I, yes. I play baseball, I dance a little too, I guess."

"There's nothing wrong with being a dancer. I'm a dancer."

"Really?"

"No. Damn, look at you, kid. You must have put up one hell of a fight."

"Yeah."

"I say we find the bastards and cut their balls off!"

"Okay."

"How did they bust your nose? Bottle? Boot heel?"

"Yeah."

"Huh? Forget it. It ain't really busted, anyway. They tagged you good though. Can you stand?"

"Yeah."

"Something smells funny?"

"Yeah, me," I said, sheepishly.

"Where are your folks? Out front? Where's your dad?"

"The hospital."

"That's who you need right now."

"Huh?"

"A doctor. Who's Patches?"

"My dog. How'd you know?"

"You said something about killing Patches."

"Oh, my mother."

"Your mother killed your dog?"

"No."

"Oh, then who?"

"The doctor."

157

"Your father killed Patches?"

"No, the vegetarian."

"Veterinarian."

"Vegetarian." Talking to Lenny wasn't easy. "Never mind. C'mon, hop in; we'll see what we can find."

"What?"

"Look behind you, down the hall. What do you see?"

"Footprints."

"Yeah and I don't want anymore. Get in. Damn kid, you stink!"

"We did that already. It's all rubbish in there."

"Paper. It'll absorb some of that, that, whatever, like kitty litter. So, what happened? They beat you; you lost control and wet yourself?"

"Okay."

Feeling, not to mention looking a little silly, I climbed in among the debris and down the hall we rolled. Like Daniel Boone, Lenny tracked my tracks.

"When we find them I suggest you file charges. But, before you do, here." Lenny reached in the dumper, taking out a billy-club. "We'll file a few charges of our own." He whapped the dumper. "We'll fix 'em. Think they can come in here?" Whap. "Do this on my watch?" Whap. "I don't think so!"

"Uh, do you think it's good idea, going four on two?"

"You held your own three on one--, I think, I thought you said three? Holy mother, this where they beat you?"

"Yeah." With the blood mixed in it looked disgusting.

"Whoa, kid, they worked you over pretty good?"

"Yeah."

"Four of them?"

"Yeah, no, three."

"It wasn't three."

"Yeah, four. Maybe five."

"How about six?"

"Yeah, six."

"How about zero?"

"Yeah, no, yeah, I dunno, why?"

"That's a lot of people, a lot of feet. I see one set of footprints. So, where's all the others? What happened? What really happened?"

Over the last twenty minutes, all hell had broken loose on stage, backstage, and in the auditorium.

Seems most people thought I had caught a good case of stage fright, ran off, and was hiding. I didn't, I really, really, didn't. Not then, anyway.

But, if I go back now and say what really happened, the truth, I'm a dead kid. If I go back with a whopper of a lie and crack, I'm a dead kid. Either way, when my mother gets her hands on me, on the bit of me left after everybody else takes their shots, she is really going to be angry. And, of course, I'm a dead kid. 'I'm not hiding, I'm surviving!' Erwin would be proud.

159

It also seems I gave Roxanne far too much credit for her creative, impromptu dance skills. Because, as rehearsed, when it came time for her (absent) partner (me) to stand over her and spin her like a top as she sat on the stage, well, she sat down on the stage alright, then, twirled herself around by the palms of her hands, around and around, all alone, while five other partnered couples spun all around her.

"You said there were three of them."

"Yeah, because you said I couldn't have done this to myself. Then you said I put up a good fight against two. Three sounded better."

And when she was to run across the stage and leap into her partner's (me) waiting (absent) arms, it didn't seem to dawn on her, if I wasn't there when she started to run and I still wasn't there when she leapt, I most certainly wouldn't be there when she landed.

"You just said you were running from them when I found you."

"No, you just said I was running from them when you found me."

When Cha-Cha realized the whole number was being laughed at, and she wasn't the center of attention, her, "The show must go on!" mentality kicked in. Much to the delight of all lovers of wildly bouncing boobs, husbands, grandfathers, uncles, etc., in attendance, Cha-Cha took a running leap, landing her patented full stretch leg split, bobbing up 'n down on her bum for effect. Cha-Cha was working her God-given magic. Well, if hooting and wolf-whistles is a good gauge of God-given magic.

"You had to go so bad you nearly knocked yourself unconscious?"

"Yeah."

Miss Colmes looked at my mother like she'd spawned the child of Satan.

"He's her son, she's even more to blame," Miss Colmes said to

Geraldine.

Geraldine could care less. She was beaming with pride. "Nine, look at my Cha-Cha. She's, ten, putting out like she's never put out, eleven, before. If only she wasn't so goddamn, twelve, shy. With all her talent I know one day she'll be a, thirteen, pro."

"Thirteen flying leg splits in a, fourteen, row? Hear those guys? As far as they care, tonight she is a, fifteen, pro!" Miss Colmes said.

"Is your dad at the hospital?"

"In, in the hospital. I know I sound like a liar but I, I—"

"Doctor?"

"Patient. The part about Patches is true though."

"Veterinarian?"

"Vegetarian."

"Veterinarian was a vegetarian?"

"I swear that part is true."

Lenny was silent. He didn't know what to make of me, or the truth, or anything. And I couldn't blame him. For a short while I actually had my miracle. An ally with an alibi. In the distance we heard the sound of a search party.

"Tell me about your dog."

"Patches? She was my other dog after No Name died."

"You named a dog, No Name?"

"Lenny, we don't have time for that story."

"That's no name for a dog."

161

"Exactly."

"So, go on."

"Oh, what? Patches? What's it matter?"

"Matters. You're running out of time. I'd talk fast."

"Well, somebody gave her to me as a puppy. Uh, I had her for about two years. Ah, she had six puppies under the house, in the crawl space. Um, one died. She was my best frien—"

"Kid, kid, sh-h, the point. Why did the vegetarian kill her? Did she attack people? Was she sick?"

"Patches or my mother?"

"You hear them? I'd say you have three, maybe four minutes. If I were you I wouldn't even breathe, just talk."

"The old guy next door, my neighbor, Cal, has this really old, squatty, low to the ground, belly draggin', arthritic crippled, leukemia riddled, deaf, blind in one eye dog, with a sac, a bulging sac hanging off his left hip, like carry-on luggage, named Amos. One day, Amos and Patches were running in circles around the yard, playing. Well, Patches was running, Amos hobbled around mostly, trying to keep up with Patches. My mother came speeding up the road and, not seeing, not looking, barreled to a hard stop in our dirt drive, paying no attention to poor old Amos who was resting from playing. I yelled to my mother, because her weight was pinning Amos under the car, "Get out of the car!"

(inhale)

She motioned for me to come to the open car window, and said, "What?" I told her she was crushing Amos, she had to get out of the car. She didn't. She reached out the window with her left hand, grabbed hold of my ear and held tight. With her right, she put the car in reverse and hit the gas. The tires spun, kicking up dirt and

162

rocks, poor old Amos got the worst of it. The car shot backwards, I fell, and she lost her hold on me. I went to Amos who was a mess, lotta dirt and little cuts. He didn't look any worse for wear, considering he'd just been run over and squashed, twice. I thought he was gonna be dead, but really, he was in pretty good shape. I was trying to stand him up when my mother charged me, grabbed a handful of my hair and led, pulled, dragged me in a willy-nilly, rag doll fashion inside the house. She pinned me against, bending me back, over the stove. "Who the fuck did I think I was yelling to the neighbors she was fat?" She's heavy, about 250-270 pounds, but tall. I never thought she was fat, just heavy. All I was trying to say was, "Get out of the car, you're too heavy!" If she did, Amos could've squirmed out, but, she didn't. She backed up, and ran over him, again! I said to her, "You ran over Amos!"

(inhale)

She looked out the kitchen window. Amos was on the grass, Patches was licking, cleaning, tending to her old friend's wounds. Cal drove by; saw Amos lying on the grass, Patches hovering over him. My mother saw Cal run to Amos. She stomped across the floor wildly, raising each leg high, slamming each step down. Her face was distorted, she pinched at it, and she kept on saying, "what'm I gonna do, what'm I gonna do, what'm I gonna do?" She turned on me, swinging an open hand. I wasn't ready. She clubbed me flush, a solid slab. I didn't see it coming, I should've known better. I ran to the living room to hide. I heard her go outside. I went to the window and saw Cal with Amos in his arms. Patches was on her hind legs, dancing around, still trying to help her fallen friend. I couldn't hear too well, but I could see Cal was doing all the talking and he was mad. All I heard him say as he walked away was, "You're damn right you'll take care of it!"

(inhale)

My mother came back in the house, told me to get Patches and wait in the car. As I went out, she picked up the phone to make a call. I got Patches and waited in the car. Finally, she came out with a paper bag and we drove away. Patches was on my lap. A few times she tried to get her nose in the bag. I saw squash, tomatoes,

163

and corn. My mother punched the bag. Patches yelped. I pulled her back to me. She snarled at my mother. "Fucking dog is dangerous!" That was all she said for the whole ride. We ended up driving a couple of towns away. She stopped at a building with a lot of trees and a high chain fence all around. We sat there. I wasn't sure what was happening. We just sat, quietly. After a while my mother gave me the bag and told me to take Patches and the bag, go in the building, and ask for (?) she didn't remember his name. I asked why and she said, "Patches needed some training so she wouldn't be so dangerous."

(inhale)

I took the bag and Patches and went inside the building. For a place working with animals it seemed quiet. Too quiet. Eventually I figured out what was really happening. I knew what was going to happen, but I didn't know why. Patches was never dangerous. Two guys were there. I didn't know who to ask for. I said I had some vegetables for the veterinarian. One guy said, "You Edna's kid?" Then he laughed and said, "I'm the vegetarian." He took the bag, I said good-bye to Patches, and went back to the car."

"And that was it?"

"Yeah, well, no. On the way home, we stopped at a pet shop."

"And she bought you a new puppy to help you forget about Patches?"

"No, she bought some fish in a plastic bag."

"Why didn't you ask her when Patches would be coming home?"

"That would've been a stupid question."

"Not in my book."

"Yeah, well, you read different books than her, I guess."

"What did your father say when you told him?"

"I didn't tell him, she did. He was pretty upset."

"She told him? Took a lot of nerve on her part, don't you think?"

"Yeah. Especially the part about the driver not stopping, just driving away after hitting Patches, leaving her dead on the side of the road. I thought that took a lotta nerve. Anyway, later, I saw my friend Reggie and he said his mother told him Patches and Amos got in a fight and Patches tore up Amos real bad."

Lenny stared down the hall at the approaching ruckus.

Miss Colmes, Geraldine, my mother, and a small Army of others approached. They were all yelling to me, at me, as they neared. I held my breath and ducked down, praying Lenny would help. He didn't say a word. He pulled the dumper over the nastiest part of the mess and I heard him walk away. He was going to let them tear me apart.

I heard loud voices and the sound of shoe heels clomping on hard tile.

The posse had their outlaw cornered.

I couldn't stand, they'd get me. Couldn't get out, they'd get me. Couldn't run, they'd get me. Couldn't breathe, that got me! I popped up, gasping for air.

Hands were reaching and grapping at me, suddenly, they drew back.

"EEEW, CHRIST! OHH MY DEAR SWEET JESUS! WHAT IN THE NAME OF HELL? I GOT THE HEAVES! URRR-URRR-URRRP!"

As they recoiled, voicing their disgust, I decided to jump out and run, anywhere, just away, this was the only way out of the mess. I looked down, ready to jump out and saw, while I was ducked down, Lenny had tracked and dragged three or four sets of

165

footprints in different directions down the hall, away from the posse.

"The kid got beat up pretty bad," Lenny said firmly, appearing from around the corner.

"Beat up? By who?" asked my mother, a tone of doubt in her voice.

"Not sure. By the look of it there had to be at least--"

"Three!" Lenny and I blurted out at the same time.

"Maybe four," Lenny said.

"I'm calling the police!" Miss Colmes said grandly.

"I already did. A couple of cruisers are outside right now seeing what they can turn up. Are you his Mom?" Lenny asked.

"What's that smell?" asked my mother, gagging.

"Him/Me," we answered in unison.

"If it's okay, I'll take him where he can clean up. We can meet you out front in about twenty minutes. Alright?"

My mother agreed, asking Lenny if he had anything to cover the car seat. Geraldine comforted my mother as they walked away.

"Why'd you do it?"

"Because."

"Patches?"

"Yeah, and nobody asked how you were."

I was embarrassed walking out front. Everyone was quietly kind as I walked past.

When we got home my mother said she was totally humiliated.

And, the beat goes on.

Chapter 13

The Blessing of the Rooms

In his new life, as in his former life, my dad befriended the most curious of characters. Two I will never forget were Fingers and Lefty.

Fingers was called Fingers because the thumb, index, and middle finger of his right hand were missing. Lefty was called Lefty because his left arm, but for a nub, was gone. At different times, this both terrified and amused me, being as my li'l black dad's name was Dick.

One day, when grousing about my given name, he delighted in telling me, with an elfin grin, how, if not for him, how close I had come to being knighted a junior. But for a frail, fragile, fateful moment of combined clarity and compassion on his part, I would have been a li'l Dick. For life.

On those days when life seems woefully bleak, I have often thought this would have been the straw which broke the camel's back.

Fingers and Lefty suggested he take up a hobby. Something to get his mind off things he could do nothing about. So, he took up painting. My li'l black dad an Artiste. 'Okay, it was paint-by-number, still it was paint.' His brush strokes though shaky at first, in time, became shaky at best.

For any, all, and every occasional gift-giving celebration,

169

disbursement of the paint-by-number treasures provided an equal, yet excessive, number of gifts for the entire family. Birthdays were popular. Followed close by Thanksgiving, Easter, Ash Wednesday and Good Friday. Leap Year, New Year, All Saints, All Souls, May, Memorial, Independence and Labor Days. Groundhog, Woodchuck, and Saint Swithens Days. But the absolute front-runner was Christmas Day.

The keepsakes arrived disguised as presents in brown paper bag wrap, secured by white surgical tape. 'Hm, I wonder? A bike?'

Out of a personal resolve to make something of his new life, and out of sheer boredom, my dad threw himself into his new found love of paint and brush with creative abandon. In almost four years since he began, hundreds, literally hundreds of paint-by-numbers made their way to my house. He was a paint-by-number machine.

They were everywhere.

Crammed in the closets. Shoved under beds. Stashed in the attic. Stored in the crawlspace. Stacked in cupboards. They were even piled in the tub. In the tub!

'Well, it's not like it was being used for anything else.'

Every inch of every wall in every room boasted paint-by-number deco.

Walk through any room in the Great White Elephant and without turning around, you could count at least a dozen paint-by-numbers of The Last Supper. Even the bathroom!

Imagine Christ and all of His Apostles, eye level as you sat, plates piled with what looked an awful lot like macaroni and cheese, gazing, glaring, staring out at you with #5 yellow, jaundice eyes. Having grown up around this just trust me when I tell you guilt and guilt alone make it virtually, humanly, entirely impossible to masturbate under this much pressure!

Even without the help of a calendar, or arrival of the yuletide trunk of paint-by-numbers for one and all, you would know the gift-giving season was nigh because at my house Christmas season was marked/marred by the visit of Father Saks, the local weeville priest.

Father Saks' yearly duty, per my mothers' request, was to visit our home a few days prior to Christmas and perform, because of the many religious themed paint-by-numbers, what became known not only up and down my dead-end street but throughout the tiny hamlet as, "The Blessing of the Rooms."

In truth, if she must hold this yuletide gala, I wanted to believe my mother's reasons were to honor my li'l black dad on the holidays by recognizing his prolific painting ability, taking stock of his ever growing, ever expanding, paint-by-number portfolio. But, in fact, I could never quite rid myself of the nagging feeling this was little more than my mother's annual convenient "One-Up-In-Your-Face" of Geraldine.

If Geraldine even hinted at the slightest bug or teeniest cough, which might cause her to beg off being by my mother's side, she could make Geraldine feel so guilty. Could a friend say no? No. And my mother knew it. The timing was not frivolous either. It was Christmas for Christ sake!

"Okay, well, that's that then." Hanky out. "I simply can't get through this alone." Sniffle. "If I am not able to call upon our friendship and your support through this, then I cancel the Blessing of the Rooms!" Blow. "And this year, there will be no Christmas! This year we cross Christ out of Xmas!" Cry on cue.

Such a Drama Queen. But, such a damn good Drama Queen.

Geraldine would bristle, yet, she always relented, always gave in. The grating on the raw nerve the "Blessing of the Rooms" caused by being held every year, and Geraldine's inability to "One-Up" it, ripped open such a chasm of resentment between the two, their ability to just get along was akin to removing an eyelash with a sledgehammer.

I would not call my li'l black dad religious, more spiritual as many
are. His philosophy was really quite simple. "Spiritual people
know what they know and they know in knowing what they know
that they know what they're content in knowing." However, on the
other hand, "Too much religion can make anybody a pain in the
arse." Simple.

One Sunday, I asked if he'd like to attend Mass at the hospital
chapel.

"I ain't been to church since Christ was a carpenter." This meant,
no. A month or so later I asked again, and he said, "No need, boy. I
seen the light."

"What?"

"Fourteen masterpieces," he called them. I held in my hands all
fourteen Stations of the Cross, done in paint-by-number. "Flip'm
fast," he said. I did. "Well?"

"What?"

"Now, flip 'em in reverse," he grinned. I did.

"Well?"

"What?"

"Seems obvious to me, the Man is getting better!" he proclaimed,
grinning from ear-to-ear at his punch line. "It's all in how you look
at it, boy."

"What?" I loved the man, but, quite frankly, he was beginning to
scare the hell outta me.

My folks never discussed religion or attended church. The only
reason my sisters and I became Catholic was the nosepicker's mom
talked my mother into it. "Sounds like a pretty good idea," said my
mother. I've no qualms being Catholic, it just seems there should

172

be more to the decision than, a "pretty good idea."

Also, on Christening Day we were 14, 11 and 8 years old, respectively. The other six or seven candidates were all under six months old. I was the recipient of a slabby slap when my mother overheard me ponder too loudly, "Who's gonna hold me in their arms when it's my turn to be anointed?"

So it seemed to me my mother's idea for the "Blessing of the Rooms" was pretty thin and came out of the blue. A stretch for a guaranteed "One-Up" over Geraldine annually.

Since the first day my dad was admitted to his second life, I'd had few chances to see him alone. However, on occasion, timing and opportunity presented itself. On one of those rare days I hitched a ride to the hospital and, against visiting hours, went to his ward to share my theory.

It was a moment, one of those rare, memorable, li'l black dad and son moments. I told him of my suspicions, my theory.

When I had finished, he told me to draw the curtain around his area. He then gave me the oddest, far-away stare. He centered his, by now, pink head on the pillow, thought a moment, then spoke.

"Boy," he said, "let me tell you something. When I was about your age, I stepped outside one Sunday into a perfect spring morning. Serenity engulfed me. The world was so quiet, the air so still, I could clearly hear a bumblebee buzzing. A whippoorwill struck up a whippoorwillian warble. I marveled at the purity. The splash of spawning herring from a nearby babbling brook lent to the virgin tranquility. The faint cry of a newborn baby added harmony to nature's choir. A breeze blew by, as soft in sound as an old soul's sigh. I felt a whispered tear rise. I felt a whispered tear fall. I glanced to the clouds and found I was looking straight to the heavens. I uttered a prayer."

"That was beauty--"

"Suddenly, the sky turned black! I fell to my knees, squashing the bumblebee! Its pricker, natures bayonet, seared into my leg! A thunderbolt hurdled down, exploding like a cannonade, blowing the whippoorwill to bits! Pieces rained into the brook, contaminating the babble, sickening the herring, poisoning the mother's milk! Then a voice, a tone-dead, lifeless, disembodied voice, rumbled down from heavens golden gate and said, "GRIN 'N BEAR IT, BOY! YOU GOT TO LEARN TO GRIN 'N BEAR IT!'"

A passing nurse heard him yell, ran over, tore back the curtain, and asked if I had any idea what a "10cc continuous morphine infusion" was?

"Yeah, I do now!"

The Blessing of the Rooms was perfect theatre. Absurd, yes, but perfect theatre of the absurd. It was perfect Christmas fare. But, above everything else, it was cast perfect by life, fate, accident, and Rudolph. By God, too, in his Divine sense of twisted humor.

Our nativity scene was strategically arranged to depict the arrival of the Three Wise Men bearing gifts of paint-by-number, to no one in particular, because the cradle was full to over-flowing with last year's paint-by-number pile.

Paint-by-number bestowing paint-by-number on paint-by-number? The meaning was lost on me.

Set across the humps of two tasseled dromedary figurines, a crudely made arrow, draped with blinking lights, pointing to my back door.

Although traffic on my dead-end street picked up considerably on the eve of my mother's Holiest of Holies showcase, no one ever stopped and came in the nut house. More cars than usual began appearing at dusk, peaking around eleven.

The caravan rolled past my house at a snail's pace. After passing they'd turn around and drive by yet again, gawking and shaking

their heads. People I didn't know. People I did know. People I didn't want to know. Parents of my classmates and classmates too, peering and pointing. Little kids pressed their noses up against the car windows like ogling little piglets, staring, as the shadowy silhouettes, eerily lit by the flicking flames of our hand-held candles, moved around inside "that" house, upstairs 'n down.

Father Saks led the room-to-room-to-room-to-room-to-hall procession, followed closely in tow by my mother, who found it necessary, for melodramatic purposes, to hold Geraldine's hand for strength, then my sisters, Grandma Millie, and me, last. Last was good. Nobody paid me any notice and the chips and cheese poopies were in abundance.

Last was not particularly good if Grandma Millie was having a bout of the "blueberries," then nobody wanted to stand downwind of Grandma Millie. I often wondered how such a small, frail, old woman could make such noises.

"You can call 'em any cute name you wanna call 'em," said my li'l black dad with a grin. "Love buttons, bon-bons, blueberries, whatever, but when the arse of the aged is blowing the notes all you can do is step aside and hum along."

I went along with this for years, with a nod and a smile. Then, one time he said it and, I don't know why, I blurted out, "I don't get it."

He didn't miss a beat. "Where're you be, let the wind blow free, boy."

"Oh, now I get it."

Every one of the paint-by-numbers was pulled from hiding from every nook and cranny and displayed. They were hung, tacked, taped, and propped up wherever space would allow. Rows, upon endless layers, upon staggered tiers, of horses, and cowboys, and campfires, and suns setting.

Flowers in vases. Flowers sans vases. All breeds of dogs and water

run colors, looking like puppies pee'd. Crucifixions to your left. Last Suppers to your right. Angels with yeast infections. Butterflies with teeth. Scenes of sailing ships and sailors, mistakes painted over by gallons of #7 sea blue-green.

It was a veritable shrinal tribute. "The World of Paint-By-Number" made all the more awe-inspiring and goose-bumpy by, "The Blessing of the Rooms."

As we scuffled room-to-room-to-room-to-room-to-hall, up the creaking stairs and down, hand held candles ablaze, Father Saks, his beanie-capped head bowed, whispered unintelligible gibberish, causing my mother's eyes to tear, nose to dripple, and her head to nod 'n bob as if she understood every word.

Geraldine bolstered my mother in loud whispers, "Be strong for Dick."

She knew I'd snicker. She knew I'd chortle. She knew I'd gulp a cheese poopie and gag. She also knew I'd catch a beating when she left. How I despised that woman!

On her last pilgrimage to "The Blessing of the Rooms," Geraldine caught my eye, shook her head, and smiled at me. It was an odd, twisted, sardonic smile. She was making a plan. Devising a scheme. I knew it. My intuition knew it. My intuition screamed it. But what? Time would tell, and in time, did it ever!

And the auto parade kept rolling by. No one stopped. No one came in.

While inside it was toasty. The oven set to a cozy 350-degree bake.

Ovaltine® flowed free. Chips and cheese poopies were plentiful.

Could Christmas get any better than this?

How 'bout Halloween?

Chapter 14

The Legal Arson

I was about to turn thirteen, my li'l black dad was about to turn
white, and Grandma Millie had taken to telling Quasimodo jokes
because of the growing hump on her back.

"Hey, bunghole, how does Quasimodo get a date on Saturday
night?"

"I dunno," I grinned, playing along. "How does Quasimodo get a
date on Saturday night?"

"Wanna hump?" And she'd smile her sweet, grandmotherly smile.

And, just about this time, the small town's powers that be,
condemned the Great Gray Monster. No fuss was made of the
town's decree, least none I recall. Geraldine, Erwin, and the brood,
just packed up late one September night and slipped away.

No hankies waved, no tears of good-bye, no, "Sorry your house got
condemned, now you gotta go," dinner party. Nothing.

The small town's "town fathers" now had a dilemma on their
hands. What to do with the eyesore, the public nuisance, the Great,
Gray, Aged Monster? The fathers called an emergency closed-door
session at Town Hall. Well, it would've been a closed-door

session, if they had a door. This was a very, very small town.

The disappearance of Geraldine, Erwin and the brood one day, then the sudden appearance of "DANGER/CONDEMNED" signs the next, jolted my world.

No more Mimi, warm, friendly smiles. See ya, Miss Congeniality.

No more Erwin, tales of his daily survival. Be strong, buckaroo.

No more Reggie. Bye, Willie-Lump-Lump.

No more Geraldine. Please!

No more Cha-Cha, blindfolds, Ponds cold cream, stick a finger in and swirl it around. Gonna miss that girl.

No more squeaking Lulu. Actually, little Lulu passed away a number of months ago. We were told Lulu's demise resulted from a build-up of pressure on her little skull. This was another half-truth. The whole truth was, Geraldine and Lulu were playing, "Who would get to Geraldine's over-stuffed sitting chair first," and, well, Lulu won, sorta. Geraldine squeaked in second. And, for a split second, that's all that was heard, "squeak!"

Lulu lay buried in land both properties shared, out behind the old shed. She was set to rest for all eternity, wrapped in a mile of aluminum foil. According to the quack vegetarian/veterinarian friend of my mother, this would supposedly encourage Lulu's preservation. And, even if so, so?

No more Chico the spider monkey and all the nasty tricks Cha-Cha trained him to do. I'd rather not go into it.

No more chaos and calamity. No more mirth and merriment. No more brilliant stupidity. Everything seemed to happen just a bit too quickly, much too quietly, and Geraldine made no attempt to "One-Up" my mother. I thought she might've been miffed no hoopla had been made over her having to move. I did feel kinda bad she'd been ignored. I was even more disappointed she didn't

give my mother one last "One-Up" for old times sake.

Then, like a ton of bricks, it hit me. Today, Geraldine and Erwin's "Great Gray Monster." Tomorrow, the "Great (formerly) White (now maroon) Elephant." My aged, dying, sagging, marooned elephant. My house. The last two year-round summer houses, gone. Like dinosaurs. Dead last of a dying breed. Extinct.

Finally, word came down. With training in mind for members of the town's all-volunteer on-call Fire Department, the "Great Gray Monster" would be razed. Burned to the ground. There would be in my very own back yard an arson. A Legal Arson! Cool. So, so cool! It's an old house anyway.

"If you look hard enough, boy, you can always find a place to hang your hat. But, a legal arson comes by once in a lifetime, if at all. I'm sorry I'm gonna miss it. It's an unforgettable experience you'll look back on in your old age. One day, boy, you might even write about it."

"I doubt it, dad."

"Remember, Rome burned while Nero fiddled."

"And that means?"

"Think about it, boy. You think about it."

Maddening, just maddening.

Geraldine and Erwin had their own unique and colorful way of managing to mismanage life's everyday ups and downs. When they had been gone a few days it dawned on me just how lifeless and pale the street had become.

Funny, occasionally hilarious, at the very least comical, and at the very, very least off the wall, Geraldine pushed the limits of good taste, smashing those boundaries to smithereens. But, because of her song, her voice, her one-woman show that night, I had to believe she had a good heart.

The legal arson fell on the ears of the potential owners as a blessing. The Great Gray Monster was of no use to them, or any other living thing as far as that goes. They were after the land for a family run business; egg farming. My new neighbors would be chicks. The gods were sticking their fingers into my funny-bone and twisting.

Geraldine's absence was affecting my mother. She was becoming more and more intolerable with every passing day. She no longer had anybody to "One-Up" or gossip with, or about. Her formidable foe and best friend gone.

When Geraldine moved into the neighborhood, Grandma Millie was pretty much left out of the Edna/Geraldine loop, so to speak. She was dropped with a sad, silent, thud. The handful of times when she was included, she was made to feel like an eccentric, geriatric, third leg. Now with Geraldine gone, my mother wanted to get back in my Grandma Millie's good graces. But, being left alone those years, while her daughter and Geraldine played at being put upon hypochondriac mothers, Grandma Millie had stopped talking to her entirely, though my mother never noticed, and had taken to talking to, and laughing hysterically at, the TV.

"God, I can't stand Groucho Marx. Here, I've got your secret word for ya, ya dirty bunghole!" she'd say, blowing a raspberry at the TV, flipping him the bird. "Red Skelton is one funny fart smella. Smart fella," she said to no one in particular one night at dinner. I smiled in my soup bowl.

"I missed the show, what was it about?" asked my mother.

"About thirty minutes," Grandma Millie said, not looking at her daughter.

Between slurps of ketchup enriched tomato soup, without raising my head, I looked at my mother sitting across from me at the other end of the kitchen table. I tried hard not to so much as grin, as Grandma Millie took my mother to task.

"What did he say that was so funny?" asked my mother, annoyed.

"What do you buy a fat cow for Christmas?" Grandma Millie asked.

My sisters, mother, and I just looked at each other.

In a deep, drawn voice, Grandma Millie said, "Moo-moo!" She threw her head back, laughing freely.

"I knew that," said my mother, "that's so old." Then a coy look came over her. My mother was going to tell a joke. "If Thumbelina marries Tom Thumb and they have kids, what would the kids be?"

"All thumbs," Grandma Millie said, not missing a beat and not laughing.

There's no other way to put it, my mother was pissed. Grandma Millie didn't care, she just kept on rolling.

"Wearing his new leather coat, guy strolls past a grazing cow, cow looks up, sniffs, says, "M-M-M-MOM?" I choked on my french fry. "Where would you send your cat to learn a trade? The Catskills!" We all giggled at Grandma Millie's silly comedy. Well, everyone but my mother. She twirled her fork in her salad and stared in her soup.

"Hear about the guy who married the perfect girl from Tulsa?" We all looked around bewildered, except my mother who was stewing in her soup. "She was dyslexic!" Grandma Millie howled. I scowled. I didn't get it. My younger sister shrugged her shoulders. She didn't get it. My mother never looked up. It was anybody's guess what she was thinking.

Finally, "Ah, I get it," said my older sister, looking at me, twirling her finger.

I knew what dyslexic meant. Unfortunately, as I pondered the problem aloud, working the word play left to right, inside out, I was not sure what, t-u-l-s-a, meant.

181

"A SLUT?" I blurted out, in the middle of a soupy slurp.

I was about to learn this was not something I was going to repeat again too soon.

As soon as I said it, all dinner chatter ceased. I looked to my mother with huge, 'I'm not sure what I just said myself,' eyes, to no avail. She gripped, then flipped, flung, threw her salad fork, destination un-chartered. The tongs struck and stuck, stabbing diagonal, hanging for a split second in front of my left eye. She stormed from the kitchen table into the living room, plopping down in Grandma Millie's favorite doily-covered chair in front of the TV.

Grandma Millie leaned over, licked her napkin, and dabbed at my cheek and eye. She was the only person on the face of the earth, who could possibly find something funny to say, at this frightening moment. "We'll pause for a minute, but be right back, after a word from our sponsor."

I dripped tears, blew nose bubbles, and gagged on a mouthful of tomato soup, all at the same time.

The legal arson was the hottest topic in town. Everywhere you went, whoever you talked to, "FIRE...FIRE...FIRE...!" Seemed like the whole town was making plans to attend or participate in some way. It got to where the town was so up for this you saw a little glow, a little spark in the eyes of a few, as they spoke with eager anticipation. Latent pyromaniacs the lot of them.

When my schoolmates realized not one of them would be blamed, accused, or even suspect, and, it was going to take place practically in my backyard, I suddenly became very popular, very popular indeed.

The few kids allowed to visit me in the past, or as their parents put it, "that kid, in that house, on that street" even requested VIP seating atop my old shed roof. "Sure, buddies."

182

Preparation for the infamous inferno began full swing, the day the Electric Company sent a crew of guys and utility trucks to my dead-end street, to kill and pull the wires. The Fire Marshall made a couple of trips to double-check the preparations to ensure a safe-burn.

The Propane Company sent workers and a baby-boom truck to remove the green "H-Bomb" which had sat on the back lawn, like a massive green Buddha, for years.

In my play-days the H-Bomb could be any given thing on any given day. A slimy-green deep-sea monster today and tomorrow, the surgically removed left testicle of the Jolly Green Giant. Our fertile imaginings knew no limits.

We called it the H-Bomb because this is what it reminded us of, not because it actually had the capability of being one. Nobody ever told us crawling, jumping, kicking, and using it for a baseball backstop could one day get us all blown to hell and back. 'If you're never told, whattya know?'

And besides, if the H-Bomb were really dangerous, why would Geraldine and my mother, when they got together for coffee and goodies, I mean gossip, why would they send us out to play on it with no warning?

"You kids go out and play nice on the H-Bomb so me and Edna can…"

"It ain't no H-Bomb, ma. It's a mass of deadly kryptonite sent from a warring galaxy far away to destroy us, and the only way we can be saved is bombarding it with these piles of rocks and glass bottles," Reggie said.

"Just play quiet and take your little sister with you," said my mother.

Two days til Dante's Inferno.

I heard my mother tell my li'l black dad, "The friggen fools who were supposed to remove the goddamn glass from the friggen hellhole never showed up. Goddamn thing's gonna be postponed for a friggen week, if not more. Fools wouldn't know their ass from their elbow!"

Translation: No Fire.

Now just hold on. I have VIP's coming. I even have a sorta, kinda, maybe, date. Kids at school who never spoke to me before will never speak to me again!

No fire? No way!

Next day, Inspectors arrived and found every pane, every shard of glass, smashed. An old broom was left leaning against the jalousie-less front door. A match box, empty, but for one unlit wooden match, set next to the broom. The Inspectors got the hint. In an hour, a truck and work crew with brooms and shovels arrived. By evening all evidence had been removed. The Festival of Flames was back on.

"I'd tell more but the statute of limitations can be very tricky."

By next mid-day the atmosphere on my dead-end street was friendly and festive; by dusk, drunk and disorderly, as the crowd swelled and the air crackled with anticipation. I wanted to scream at them all, "Doesn't it bother any of you a family had to lose their home to bring you all togeth--?" 'Oh, phuck it.'

It was warm for late November. With the full moon all a-glow like a Harvest Moon, it looked and felt more like fall.

Because the Great Gray Monster's property lines abutted the woods on two sides, and because of the dozen or so old elm and maple trees which had taken root on the property generations ago, and because no one had been living there for the last two months to rake, a thick, dense, bed of dead leaves, cushiony to the step, carpeted the property. The only exception was where the weeville town workers had pulled a good amount of leaves away from the

structure for safety measures, creating a pretty big snaking mound of dead leaves around the perimeter of the property.

I stood atop the old shed roof awaiting my VIP's. Looking down off the sloped-edge to the ground, I thought about all the dead dogs, birds, hamsters, and guinea pigs buried there. I could recall all their names, but the list would be as long as your arm. My li'l black dad once joked, "Confucius say, never name your pets. This makes eating them much easier." He was trying to be funny. We never really ate them. Although, now as I think of it, the beef stew did taste a little gamey from time to time.

The one animal we had that died, the one animal not represented, remembered, or given a behind the shed burial, was Queenie, an old cataract cursed horse, given to my older sister to care for. Funny how I did all the yuck stuff that came along with the tending of such an animal, but she got all the credit for its care, and, she was the only one allowed to ride it.

The one and only time I was allowed on Queenie, was when I made enough of a pest of myself to have my mother insist my sister take me along with her, when she rode Queenie to the small town store about a mile away. No sooner had we arrived at the two-lane main road, when my sister told me to, "Turn around completely, and don't ask any questions!" So I ended up facing backwards. Then she slapped her heels against Queenie's sides and off Queenie ran, with my sister doing her very best Sheba, Bareback Riding Bimbo act.

Meanwhile, I'm lying flat on the horse's sweaty, slippery, stinky rump, clutching at anything, finding nothing, but the occasional lucky snag of Queenie's wildly swishing tail, which I tried holding on to for dear life. With every jarring clappity-cleppity-clippity-cloppity-cluppity-clappity-cleppity-clippity-cloppity, my little butt shot skyward one second, then came slamming, crotch crashing down on Queenie's bulbous back the next. Oncoming traffic slowed in total disbelief, staring at me. Then they either pointed, waved, laughed, or all three!

The one thing, the one single common denominator every one of

those car jockeys had, was the nauseous ability to scream out horse's ass jokes at me, while many of them made wolf-whistles at my sister who rode staunch and upright, her bouncing, perky titties pointing to the setting sun. Certainly Patty must be the adopted one.

Acts of humiliation trip everyone up from time to time, this is a simple fact of life. But, these, these moments were becoming an everyday way of life.

A few years back my Grandma Millie got quite sick. I don't know what was wrong. I overheard my mother on the phone say, "There's chance she's not going to make it." Innocently, I asked my li'l black dad if I could dig out by the shed under the shade of the old elm tree.

"For what?"

"To bury Grandma Millie."

He grinned and said, "I don't see why not, boy. She ain't my mother."

This sounded like an OK to me.

The dig was going pretty well, til my mother asked, "What in the name of hell are you digging?"

With an achy back and sweaty brow, I said in fact, "Your mother's grave."

She dragged me outta that hole, smacking me from the backyard right through the porch screen and kitchen doors. My li'l black dad sat in his chair watching the Sox. I passed by dodging, ducking every two out of three blows. He gestured to me as if to say, "Christ, boy, I didn't think you'd actually start diggin'!"

I could see just about everyone from atop the shed roof. I kept watching for my kinda, sorta, maybe, date. I spotted my first VIP. A few minutes later another, then another, they seemed to arrive in

186

intervals. One-by-one. As each straggled in, they spoke of having just seen her, so I knew she was near. This is to be my night of passage. Every kid in town knew her. Tonight, I get to know her.

Geraldine and Erwin's misfortune was a rousing success. Everybody who was anybody, and a whole lot of nobodies, showed up. All of dinky town's bored members and bored officials, and even smaller boring politicians, worked the crowd. Slapping backs, shaking hands, puffing stogies, laughing and posturing.

All the townies were there, grouped in their private little pockets, kibitzing about other townies standing no more than a few feet away, grouped in another tight little pocket, talking about the other towni..., well, you get the idea, while their kids romped and tunneled amidst the massive, snaking, pile of leaves.

My mother stood there eyeballing them all, with her all too familiar piqued look on her face. These were the same people who, every year, gawked and drove right by. Who never once attended the blessed Blessing of the Rooms.

'The bastards!' I could hear it in her glare.

All my dead-end street neighbors were there, a ton of townies and a smattering of strangers. Some guy with no arm and his fingerless buddy.

"Hey, Fingers, Lefty. Up here, guys!"

"Wanna beer?" Lefty yelled.

"Nah, maybe later."

Having a beer with them would never happen, but the look on my VIP's faces made me feel so cool.

Thanks, Fingers. Thanks, Lefty.

Father Saks was in attendance. On the one hand it seemed a little odd, on the other, why not? I just knew his next Sunday sermon

would have something to do with, "rising from the ashes," "fire and brimstone," or, "if you can't stand the heat, don't dally in the devil's kitchen," or, well, you get the idea there, too.

My mother quickly cornered Father Saks. Mrs. Snot wouldn't dare ask her for money now. Damn, I gotta admit, she is good.

Finally, the moment arrived. The Fire Chief took a matchbox from his pocket. The slurred murmur of the crowd went silent. He shook the box. One wooden match dropped out onto his hand. He glanced suspiciously about the crowd looking for a face which might have an all over guilty look. Then he dashed the match against the striker and, turning the matchbox, he lit the box on fire. He let it fall to the paper and debris. The Chief backed away as tiny flickers darted quickly from the pile, shot across the kitchen floor, and up the walls. The silent tongues licked and lashed, biting hard into the dry, aged wood, and in an instant, whoosh, flames waved and danced from every window on the first floor.

The Pyromaniacs Pyrotechnic Party was officially underway. The crowd roared unanimous.

"YEAH!" Then, "YEAH!" again.

The massive building gave out a second, whoosh, and the entire Great Gray Aged Monster was totally engulfed. There was a tremendous surge of cracks, snaps, and pops. Millions of tiny embers, like fireflies, danced on the night sky stage, daring to out-sparkle the twinkling stars, in the backdrop of the Harvest Moon. A perfect setting for--?

I was beginning to wonder if my sorta, kinda, maybe, date, was ever going to show.

The distant sound of a car backfiring caught everyone's attention. As the distraction grew closer we all wondered the same thing, "Who the hell?"

The late afternoon dusk made it hard to immediately distinguish just who was crashing the town folk's private pow-wow. Finally,

the vehicle came into view. It pushed grudgingly forward, guided by one headlight, gears grinding, tailpipe dragging.

The definitive bucket of bolts rounded the corner of the dirt road beside my house, heading straight for the festivities, kicking up dirt, dust and stones in its wake.

A battered, beaten Buick, U-Haul trailer in tow, came into view. Finally, it gave one last lurch and died in place. The car doors flung open. Out stepped Erwin and the brood. Then, Geraldine. Geraldine!

I knew she'd be back. I just knew it. But, why? Why? Why?

"Why?"

Because, Geraldine had set a One-Up in motion months ago. A One-Up my mother would never, ever, even on her best day, equal.

Geraldine dislodged herself from the Buick, leaned forward, and pressed onward. From the look on her face, this was a woman on a mission. The flames from her once, Home Sweet Home, now, Hell's Halfway House, lit up her search and destroy features. She swiped at the ash and thick smoke that landed on and swirled about her sweaty face, while pawing aside gray clumped strands of her long lost Dutch cut.

She plodded down the path the crowd cleared getting out of her way.

"Looking neither left nor right but arrow straight, her prey caught in the crosshairs. She spoke not. Not spoke back." (Hood, Robin CBS 1962)

She stopped, right where the rim of the crowd stood closest to withstanding the intense heat, and raised-up her ham-hock size floppy arms. Her daisy dotted muumuu rose up a bit too high, showing way too much thigh, this is when I closed my eyes.

Daring to squint, it looked as if she was about to bow in worship to

the Devils Deity. But, as I opened my eyes wider, having spied her quarry through the flaming house a-fire, she began waving her arms. Everything about her rolled in waves. Her waves seemed to wave right back at her.

My mother gave a half-hearted wave, unsure why, or even if she was the target of Geraldine's show of glee. Father Saks yapped away at my mother's ear oblivious to the pending fiasco. Geraldine was on the move, trudging along the rim of the fiery arena. My mother kept her in sight, nodding as Father Saks rattled on, as if all was fine.

Geraldine was heading my mother's way, her arms rising slowly as she neared. My mother, thinking she was going to be greeted with a hug, raised up her arms and just at the last moment when the two would have met and greeted as old friends, Geraldine reached out, snagged Father Saks by the crook of his arm, whisked him from my mother, and walked on. Stunned, my mother stood there, arms extended, looking the fool. Seizing the opportunity, Mrs. Snot closed in on my mother.

So, on a typical New England Harvest Moon November eve, as billowy smoke plumes signaled the Heavens, as a gazillion ember fireflies played tag with twinkling stars, as the innocent folks of smallville mulled over the same thought at the very same time, "Shit, we shoulda brung some weenies!" Geraldine readied to let loose the Mother Of All One-Ups.

All was not well in tiny town and it ain't getting any better.

Chapter 15

The Blessing of the House

Uncle Jay and Aunt Judy have been on my mind a lot lately. He, or she, or either one of them, would have gotten a kick out of the gala. Then this morning, out of the blue, a package arrived for me. The return name, Charles Atlas, neatly written in the upper left hand corner. Had Uncle Judy or Aunt Jay, whichever, sent in a coupon? I had to chuckle. I tore at the box. The Golden Rose fell out. The attached note simply read, "Staying with friends. See you in three to five. Love, J."

In one fell swoop the bush had become a scrub.

Reggie told me Geraldine knew about the condemning of the Great Gray Monster as far back as last Christmas. This explained the look she gave me at the last Blessing of the Rooms. Geraldine was planning way back then. I knew it. This is how I knew she'd return. I just knew it!

So, when the date for the Burning of the Boonies was set, Father Saks was contacted by Geraldine to perform, as the home-fires were fully ablaze, a rather odd, never heard of benediction. As the folks of weeville stood silent, heads bowed, Father Saks, with Geraldine at his side, dutifully performed, "The Blessing of the House."

Once again, "The Blessing of the House!"

My mother was unable to accept with grace Geraldine's major in your face "One-Up."

She was polite enough to keep her seething anger in check during the informal solemn ceremony, she put up a good front, but she was furious. Let's face it; she only had the Blessing of the Rooms.

Geraldine had Father Saks, whose very presence gave the evening a bona-fide religious stamp. She had the heated excitement of a blistering inferno shooting like a geyser to the Heavens, blasting straight up from the bowels of Hades. And, she had an audience of uncountable proportions. And, to top it all off, she was offering up a whole house. Not just a trite blessing of a room or two, but the blessing of a whole house! And not just any old year-round, run of the mill, summer house either but, "The Great Gray Monster!"

My mother's reaction was typically ridiculous. First she beckoned my younger sister Liz, who I hadn't heard speak at all for the last few weeks. Not since my mother threw out my sister's red plastic telephone where the voice of her once imaginary friend had lived for years. When her red plastic telephone disappeared, so did her invisible friend. I felt bad when I saw the phone had been thrown out. It was beginning to have the creepiness of a good "Twilight Zone" episode.

My younger sister's not speaking was not from a lack of ability to express herself, she just never had to. My older sister finished her thoughts, my mother finished her conversations. My mother even offered opinions on how Liz felt on her behalf. Liz could speak; she just never had the chance.

Next my mother called my older sister Patty, who had supposedly been playing hide-n-seek in the darkness of the woods with Cha-Cha and Mimi. This struck me as a rather odd game for her to be playing, considering her age. I thought I had glanced Patty's old boyfriend lurking in the wood line earlier, but I wasn't positive. If he was here, somewhere, he was hiding from my mother. Finally, when Patty emerged from the woods, all disheveled, with a ripped

condom wrapper stuck to the back of her sweater, I was sure he was and positive they had.

Then my mother signaled me off from atop the old shed roof where I waited patiently, still standing a lonely sentry's vigil, watching for my sorta, kinda, maybe, date.

Lastly we found Grandma Millie standing with Cal. She was talking, not necessarily with Cal, but talking nevertheless, about how closely she identified with poor ol' Amos, and how the pitiful dog's aging ailments and maladies were not all that far removed from her own.

"Every beautiful thing that lives and breathes, sooner or later dies and rots," she'd say, catching any one person or an entire congregation off guard. My mother pulled Grandma Millie away just as she was about to explain to Cal her abstract theory on how the sac which hung off of ol' Amos' hindquarter was not all that far removed from the hump on her back.

And as all the nosey noses stared, townies, neighbors, VIP's, strangers, et al, my mother trooped us away from the festivities, back to my house. Under orders, we took an armful each of the paint-by-number heirlooms which had, over the years, grown around us like stalagmites, in stacks and piles of varied height. They leaned, tilted, and fell on each other around every room.

My mother was not about to go down in front of the teeny town folks, let alone Geraldine, without a fight. And she had no qualms, no qualms whatsoever, taking us down with her.

I now wished my kinda, sorta, maybe, date, would never show up.

Armed with a dozen or more paint-by-numbers each, which scarcely made a dent compared to what was left, we traipsed back towards the Devil's Weenie Roast laden with art forms. But for the fiery glow three house lots ahead, and the now smoke-shrouded Harvest Moon, it was very dark. I took this as a sign, a blessing. I didn't have to look anyone in the eye.

Thank God for little favors.

Shadows danced everywhere. At a short distance, as we passed the old shed. My VIP's stood and waved at me with their bottles of be--! I wanted to yell out, "Hey, who in hell said anything about beer?" I wanted to yell, but my mother beat me to it. The only difference is, she did not yell at them, she yelled at me. Then, she looked at me. This was all she had to do. 'I'll deal with your little ass later,' is what her look said. When she knew her glare had done its job she, thank Christ, snapped her look away from me and back to the sorry soiree. I felt blessed for a second because, just as she looked away, Fingers popped up from behind my VIP's and gave a silly, drunken salute.

'Well, that explains the beer,' I grinned.

In the flickering shadows, off the furthest side of the shed roof, Lefty was relieving himself. He had his beer bottle tucked under his left nub, and using his right hand for steady streamline guidance, which, like my li'l black dad's brush strokes, was shaky at best, he teetered and slowly wavered. Hearing his buddy Fingers salute me, Lefty turned to salute also. By normal reaction, his left nub shot up for balance and his beer bottle fell from the nub's hold, hitting the head of a VIP! Lefty spun around and tried to bend down where he had heard the thunk and loud groan.

A sharp, quick, clearly distinct, female yelp rang out, and by the light, by the dim light of the Harvest Moon, and the rage of the Great Gray Monsters pyre, I saw the outline of a female wiping her topless self dry.

'Oh, if this isn't a kick in the head. My kinda, sorta, maybe, date, made it after all. Unfortunately, however, it wasn't me she was making it with!'

Words from my dear li'l black dad's book of tortured wisdom reverberated in my head, 'It's a mighty fine line between a ponytail and a horse's arse!'

None of this is my fault, or is it?

In a bizarre, perverse, twisted bit of foolish, friggen fate, I have become a reluctant player in this, the Mother Of All One-Ups! 'I wanted you to have a, sorry your house got condemned now you gotta go, dinner party! You great, huge, whopping, crazy lady!' Strike 1.

I also missed out on my first sure thing. 'I never had a sure thing in my life! First or otherwise! I never even had a thing!' Strike 2.

And last, I know before this night is over, I just know, 'I am gonna get such a beating!' And none of this, I repeat, none of this is my fault! Strike 3! Yer out!

Let the friggen good times roll!

On one side of Hell's Hothouse stood Father Saks, Geraldine, Erwin, the brood, and half of itsyville. On the other side stood, my mother, Grandma Millie, my sisters, me, and the other half of bitsyville. At our feet, at the ready, approximately eighty paint-by-number treasures to be sacrificed

In time, the all-volunteer, on-call firemen gathered up the weaponry, less one hidden by my mother, and threw them to the fire.

Residents of the hamlet of horrors would refer to the evening for months to come as "The Blessing of the House" featuring "The Blessing of the Paint-By-Numbers." A sorta double billing.

Only when the massive, intricately woven mish-mash of raven charred timbers with fireflies spewing, damn, vomiting, cracked, and let out a long, brutal, beastly, monsterishly dying, rrroooaaarrr, and caved, and not until the last remaining member of the all-volunteer on-call Fire Department was extricated and accounted for, did anyone even think about leaving.

As the occasional firefly ignited hotspots dotting the scarred Chinese dragon looking leaf pile were watered down, the Townies carefully dug their children out and began exiting. Some shook

their fists, most yelled vague obscenities, and all, at one moment or another, displayed fleeting talents for finger puppetry and unique and creative abilities in sign language.

Not until she felt in her devious soul it was the right, the exact, the infinitesimally perfect moment, did Geraldine drop the gauntlet, lower the boom, lance the juggler, and go in for the kill.

Like a mother sow to her sucklings, Geraldine called her brood to her side, and against Father Saks' righteous pleas, raised her arms for silence, and in a most mournful tone led a final Holy. "God is great. God is good. Let us thank him, for this wood. Aaaamennnn."

'Well, that explains the trailer,' I thought.

My mother, rising to the challenge, knowing it better to secede to a TKO than succumb to a full scale KO, threw in her two cents. Like Geraldine, she ignored Father Saks' pleas, gathered her litter near, got down on her knees, and chimed in with her clearly garbled, Holiest of Holies entry.

"Mother Mary Fuller face, the Lord's on TV, dressed in his Fruit of thy Looms, please us. Pray for us winners now and then. Amen." I swear, those very words came out of her mouth!

Then, grinding her heel in his soul for the part he played in Geraldine's ingenious "One-Up," my mother insisted Father Saks bless the last held paint-by-number. I know I heard the word "blasphemous" through his mumbling. My mother set it a-sail with enough wrist flip for it to slice the top off a mountain of glowing embers, coming out on the other side, scattering the older, slower stragglers, striking Mrs. Snot right in her Avon tote bag.

Father Saks made his leave raving about God's wrath.

The one lasting memory I took home of the Great Gray Monster that night, was the sight of Geraldine and Erwin's old ball-and-claw bathtub, precariously perched, teetering on a flame consumed second floor. When the old ball-and-claw finally tried coming down, it broke through the second floor feet-end first, then slid,

stopping for a brief moment, held back from its fiery plummet by plumbing fixtures at the faucets end.

The torched floorboards soon gave way to the vessels weight. Then a sick, twisting, metal ripping screech and groan, as the cast iron Rudolph wanna-be appendage tore free of old metal and brass veins and arteries, pulling the interior wall down with it, crash landing in the exact spot where their old living room sofa once sat. I winced at the words of my mother's year in, year out warning, of our tub crashing down onto our living room sofa.

I glanced back up at the exposed wall. Not a hint of insulation. At least my Great White Elephant protected the Great Gray Monster all these years from the bone chilling winds of the East Lake, for what it was worth.

A glint, a single sparkle of something much more brilliant than the fiery flaming flashes surrounding it, caught my eye. It just hung there, occasionally licked by the firestorm, sparkling once again. It took a few minutes then it began, slowly, tipping forward, wavering, as if taking a slow, low, final bow, then, broke free. Straight down it came, careening off the edge of the cast iron tub, hurtling in an arc in my direction, landing like a smoking gun at my feet. I stared at the object in disbelief. It was a smoking showerhead. For all these years, the Great Gray Monster had a shower!

'I never knew!' I thought, staring.

'I would've bet money.' I grinned, amused.

'If you're never told, whattya--' I tried to reason.

'Shut the phuck up!' I yelled, silently.

The last I saw of Geraldine, Erwin, and the brood that night, they were loading the trailer with still smoldering bits and pieces of the Great Gray Monster, for memories sake, for keep sake, "To burn in their fireplace for Christ sake," as my mother put it.

At this point, it would be perfect for me to say that on the way home, their trailer caught fire, burning right there on the main road. But this just didn't happen. This would be fiction. This would be a lie.

The last memory I have of my mother that night was assisting her to stand erect, having lost her balance attempting to genuflect.

A few days later, I hitched a ride to the hospital to make a visit. Fingers and Lefty would have already told my dad about the Great Gray Monster, my VIPs, my sorta, kinda, maybe, date, and all. 'So, it's an uneventful visit. Still, it's a visit.'
I pushed through the wards double-wide swinging doors, just as he was wheeling himself out.

"Be right back, boy."

"I'll go with ya."

"Go in, go in, two minutes," and off he rolled.

I walked down to his area nodding to those who waved or looked at me.

Even after these first few years, I never really talked to anyone. Some always had visitors, some spent their time in therapy, or the day room, or slept, or silently wept.

The curtain around his area was drawn almost shut. I looked in and immediately noticed the area empty of all his personal belongings. Nothing. Nothing at all. Not a hint of my li'l black/Caucasian dad's existence existed. I stepped in the enclosure and stood there. Was he coming home? I was at a loss.

Not knowing what else to do but wait, I sat on the edge of the tautly made bed.

After a short moment my antsiness and curiosity got the best of me. I opened the cabinet to his bedside stand. Empty. 'What's going on?' I opened the drawer and lying face-up, unfolded,

unwrinkled, in my li'l black/Caucasian dad's handwriting was a note, a letter of sorts, with no name as to who it was for.

"I'll die soon. Maybe I already have. Maybe this afternoon. Or yesterday morning. Or tomorrow night. Or as you're reading this. It will be quick, subtle. Maybe. Maybe not.

Death can be a sneak. Still, I hope I see it coming. Why? Maybe this is the secret. Turn the tables. Surprise death before death surprises you. Seize the opportunity before death seizes you. And when, look the Reaper square, and say, 'Not now. Not yet. I have people to love. Children to listen to. Hugs to get. To give. Tears to wipe. To fall. No. Not today. Not now.'

Find a way to love, complete, before death cuts in, absolute. If I'm not on my guard I may die before I write the last lette...

Nope. Not then. Not yet. False alarm. Sorry. Hope I didn't give you a heart attack. We may meet before the final second. Or during. Don't worry. I doubt it. But, are you ready? Would you stand by me? Or stand by? It's okay. We all have to go someday."

I stood staring at the letter. Was this yet another example of a 10cc continuous morphine infusion? I was lost in thought when, "OW-W!" My li'l black/Caucasian dad rode his wheelchair right up behind me, the foot pedal dug into my upper heel. I hobbled as I turned, falling onto the bed.

"What're you doing over here? They moved me over there," he said, pointing through the curtain, up the aisle, to a bed on the other side of the ward.

"Oh, I didn't know." I was bleeding slightly, being cut, getting rammed. "What's this?"

"What?" He took it, recognized it, rolled it in a ball, dropping it in the ashtray set on his blanketed lap. "Nuttin."

"Nothing? But, it's your writing."

"Some new guy had the bed for a few days. He wanted to meet a nurse."

"Like, a girlfriend?"

"Whatever."

"But, you wrote it."

"I did. He copied it, gave it to her, she gave it to his doctor, they put him in the nut ward." He lit a Salem®, grinned wide and exhaled.

"Poor bastard."

"No, really? But, they're your words."

"They are. They think it sounded suicidal."

"It's good."

"Yeah, if you're suicidal. So, what's up, boy?"

"That's it?"

"He'll be back in a week or two."

"Nothing else?"

"That's it. It's none of your bees-wax, boy."

"Did you hear about the fire?"

"Yeah. How's your girlfriend?"

"Oh, she's not my girlfriend. The night didn't go the way I planned."

"Never do. She doesn't sound special. What are you looking for, boy?"

"Huh?"

"I heard about the one in the dance class, she was seeing somebody. Now this new one sounds like she's seeing everybody. You're almost thirteen, boy, what are you looking for? What do you like?"

"Where?"

"In a woman."

"I dunno." I was stumped. "What'd you look for? What do you like?"

"Where? In a woman?"

"Yeah."

"Me!" he said, grinning his broadest grin. He didn't call it back or nothing. It was like he was talking to one of the guys.

"Dad!"

"It's a joke, boy. It's a joke. Don't repeat it."

"Can I tell Grandma Millie?"

"Where you think I heard it?" We laughed. "Don't tell your mother."

"I hear that a lot."

"Yeah, well, boy, it ain't easy. You got clothes on your back, a roof over your head, three squares a day, yeah? Whattya want for nothin'? Somethin'?"

"No," I said, even though I had no idea what he meant.

"Your day'll come, boy. Wait your turn."

"Whattya mean?"

"Food for thinkin'," he grinned. "Push me to the dayroom. Cribbage match in five minutes."

This would have been the perfect time to try to tell him what my life had turned into since he left. But, I couldn't do it. Anyway, something told me he knew. What good would it do to put it into words? Nothing could be done about it.

I rolled him through the ward, out the swinging double doors, down the length of the green gloomy hall, past the nurse's desk and main entrance, to the open dayroom doors in silence. He waved to his waiting wheel-chaired buddies. "See ya later," I said, patting his shoulder. For some reason, for no reason, this had been a quick, somewhat sad visit. I couldn't put my finger on just why, but something had changed. 'He only knows what he's told,' I thought. 'What's she telling him?'

"How'd you get here?" he asked. I stuck up my thumb as I walked to the main entrance. "Always works. I was thinking about your problem."

"What problem?" I said turning, leaning against the doors.

"Women," he said, and we both smiled.

"How's that?"

"Better to find the Beauty in the Beast than the Beast in the Beauty."

"Not bad. Confucius?"

"No. Me, boy. Me!" he said, grinning from ear-to-ear. He stuck his cigarette in his mouth, grasped the skinny, over-sized wheels of his chair and rolled away.

I pushed against the heavy doors and stepped into a warm November sun, a chilly November wind. Looking down the twenty or so steps to the walkway, I suddenly felt like Jimmy Cagney in "Yankee Doodle Dandy." The scene where his character, George M. Cohan, leaves the meeting with the President and tap dances down the spiral staircase to exit.

No one was looking. I gave a small hop, landing lightly on the first step down. I gave a second push off, landing on the second step just as lightly as the first, but the back of my shoe pushed up into the cut where the foot pedal had bit me. My knee buckled, I lurched forward, tumbling down five or six steps.

I quickly righted myself with the help of the rail and looked about. No one saw a thing. I brushed myself off as I limped down the remaining steps. My white sock was turning blood red. It was a long walk off the hospital grounds to the main road. I thought I heard a woodpecker, or something of the sort, tapping behind me. Looking back, watching me through the large dayroom window, shaking his head and grinning, was my li'l black/Caucasian dad.

What? Why was he grinning? Beauty in the Beast? My time'll come? Clothes, a roof, three squares? There's got to be more to it than that. There has to be. I'll figure it out. I'll be back, come hell or high water. Whatever that means. When I figure it out, I'll be back.

I smiled, waved and, as I hobbled away, Grandma Millie came to mind, 'Look at the little bunghole will ya. Clear as mud. Confused as ever.'